Pamela was born in Dagenham, Essex in 1938; the following year, war broke out. Sadly, her school, one mile from the River Thames, was badly bombed. Therefore her proper schooling was started when she was seven years old with the playground still full of rubble. Happier times came when Pam joined the Kitty Harris Stage School of Dance, where she excelled. She married, moved to Devon in 1963, bought a guest house and had three daughters. In 1973, she and her husband sold up and moved to a cottage with two acres, opening the gardens for charity. In 1999, they retired to a bungalow overlooking the sea, opening the gardens again. In 2019, they celebrated their 60th wedding anniversary with 140 guests, in the guest house they used to own. (It is now the high-class Best Western Hotel, and is still haunted.)

To my small writing group of skilled friends that allowed me to join them so that they could keep an eye on me: Jenny, Jill, Carol, Louise and Jeanie.

My very precious friend in Palm Cove, Australia, a published writer who gave me guidance and stopped me from falling into the pitfalls. I'm ever grateful. Thank you, Kay Crabbe.

Pamela Florence Martin

HIGHLAND HERITAGE

AUSTIN MACAULEY PUBLISHERS™

LONDON * CAMBRIDGE * NEW YORK * SHARJAH

A CIP catalogue record for this title is available from the British Library.

ISBN 9781398420977 (Paperback)
ISBN 9781398422711 (Hardback)
ISBN 9781398422728 (ePub e-book)

www.austinmacauley.com

First Published 2022
Austin Macauley Publishers Ltd®
1 Canada Square
Canary Wharf
London
E14 5AA

I would like to thank Austin Macauley Publishers for their skilled help.

Chapter 1

Helen Glenkerry dangled her feet in the gently flowing burn. The cool water lapped around her ankles bringing childhood memories clear and colourful, as she watched the thin green water grasses curve about her toes. At ease with her beloved glen and breathing a sigh of contentment, she lowered her hands into the water, studying the array of pebbles then splashing her face, it's just too beautiful, enjoying the cold beads of water trickling down her neck and into the curve of her breast.

As far as the eye could see were mountains tinged with a bluish haze and green hills and valleys with the breeze bringing the sweet smell of heather. Helen rolled her white cotton trouser legs up a bit further and reaching for the bank where her sandals lay pulled a lace out of one of them scooping her shoulder-length hair high on her head, tying it firmly, then moved another step more into the burn. Although the water was icy, a warmth filled her. "Oh, Aunt Matty, I will look after it. I will love it just as much as you did, thank you, thank you."

Sitting now on the edge of the burn, she lay slowly back feeling the grass cushioning her body as the rippling water caressed the backs of her legs making music as it bent the reeds and weaved around the boulders.

Reflecting now that she must have been out for quite a while and it was going to be a long walk back to her aunt's lodge, she had better make a start, knowing she had followed no particular route. Picking up her sandals and smiling at having all this to herself except for the bird's song, 'oh, such carefree abandonment', she reluctantly stood up. Her feet were beginning to feel a little numb as she stepped out of the water.

Slowly surveying the scenery enjoying one last look, she could just make out a horse and rider in the distance. Watching she noticed the horse walking at times then galloping at speed to disappear behind some trees. Helen had the feeling that the rider must be looking for something or someone. Now they were a little nearer losing them in the contours of the hills. So she didn't have it all to herself, letting her gaze go into infinity. Stepping out of the water, she sat herself on a long smooth boulder pushing her wet foot into her leather sandal sat there looking at it. Aunt Matty had bought them for her a few years ago on one of Helen's visits to her aunt's Scottish home; she left them here deliberately. Now she treasured them.

The memories came drifting back, the summers, the fun, the laughter and family gatherings; she had spent most of her school holidays here. Sighing as her sandal came back into focus, she turned to reach for the other sandal. With a start, she saw the horse was standing motionless a little way from her, its rider watching her. They moved slowly forwards.

Helen felt a wave of fear; she was a long way from anywhere. Clutching her sandal, she started to roll her trouser legs back down while keeping an eye on the rider. Now she was looking at his hooves close to her own feet and could feel its breath on her hair. Having done some riding herself, she wasn't too put out by the horse. It was a lovely animal with a glossy body and as she stood up had to stop herself from gasping. The man seated in the saddle as if he had been moulded there made a handsome pair.

His look was penetrating as he raised his head, his dark hair outlined against the sky, his expression stern. Helen shielded her eyes from the brightness of the sky as he lent forward in the saddle. "Don't you know it's dangerous for a young girl to be out this far on her own?" Startled at the sudden harshness in his voice, she took a step backwards but looked him full in the face. This time, she did have to catch her breath at the sheer good looks of this man still looking crossly down at her. In an instant, she realised she must have looked much younger than her twenty-two years and decided to try a friendly approach.

Smiling up at him, she said, "Hallo." His expression was still dark.

"This is McKlinross land and you, young lady, are trespassing."

Slipping the sandal off and throwing them onto the burn edge deliberately keeping her back to him, she waded into the middle of the water, giving an involuntary shiver as she did so, then turned to look back at him. Her heart missed a beat. His expression had softened, as he looked about him slightly puzzled. "Where have you come from, and where do you think you are going?" Helen thought for a moment as she rolled a pebble along the bottom of the burn with her toes.

Putting her hands on her hips and lifting her chin, she calmly enquired, "Why who wants to know?" His eyes narrowed momentarily, but there was a fleeting smile on his lips.

He nodded and said, "James." Then waited.

"Helen and I'm at the lodge with Aunt…" She was almost going to say Aunt Matty. Aware of the lump in her throat and tears not far away.

Picking up her sandals and thinking to herself, her aunt would have known this man, she knew all the glen folk. The unshed tears burned at the back of her eyes, and she turned away. "The lodge you say?" She nodded without looking at him. He moved the horse alongside her and extended his arm leaning forward. "Here, I'll take you back on Cavalier." She backed away.

"No, it's—"

But he repeated, "Here," still holding his arm out. "I want you off this land and back safely where you belong." Helen felt a niggle forming again; she noticed the crest on his saddle blanket and recognised it. He must be in the employ of a landowner here.

His horse stood like a rock as James swung her effortlessly up behind him immediately firmly pulling both her arms around him. Turning his head towards her and for a second time that day her heart skipped a beat. "Hold tight, it might be a bumpy ride in places, comfortable." She felt him take her sandal from her and slide it into the front of his top.

There was a surge of power beneath them, and Helen felt dismay as she caught a glimpse of the other lace-less sandal still on the side of the burn. As her hair streamed out in the wind, she made up her mind she would be back for her other precious sandal and tried to take in clues of the location, but it wasn't easy with her head pressed against the middle of his back and in full gallop. Somehow, she felt quite safe with this man; it wasn't something she would have done in London, be so trusting as to be picked up by a stranger.

The glen passed in a blur of green; she knew at one point they had jumped the burn; they seemed to float for a second, as she felt him cover her hand firmly. Her hair streamed out, the sandal lace long gone as she clung to this stranger. Lifting her head as the pace had slowed, she began recognising the contours of the land and the rise ahead knowing the lodge would soon be in sight. Helen felt a slight sadness this experience would soon be over.

They had slowed now to a walk, and she was aware of him stroking the horse's neck and speaking to him in soft tones. His hands looked strong but gentle, and for a moment, Helen wished it was her, then blinked at herself in surprise. This wasn't a bit like her at all. Sitting up straight now, she loosened her grip around his waist. He turned with a quick smile. "All right back there?" She nodded, returning the smile. Still stroking he said, "Well done, Cavalier."

The horse's easy stride had made smooth going of the many rough outcrops, and now she was enjoying the feel of its silky body rubbing rhythmically against her bare feet. Every now and then, Helen could see the lodge over James's shoulder and just make out her aunt's lifelong friend Mary talking to her husband Angus in the rose garden.

Feeling her throat tighten at not being able to see her beloved aunt, she swallowed hard and unconsciously rested her head against James's back. The hollow was there again of an empty space inside her, then she realised they had stopped. Feeling him turn towards her slipping his arm under her shoulder, gripping her and lowering her to the ground. For one wonderful moment, a mass of dark hair touched her face and the tantalising aroma of freshly washed hair, then she was sliding down the horse's flanks and her feet were on the ground. It had happened so quickly that she had instinctively grasped some of his clothing. His face still close to her, he smiled looking at her hand. "You can let go now." Although he still had hold of her arm.

Looking back up, she was surprised to see how far off the ground she had been. Suddenly feeling shy, she said 'sorry' as he uncurled her fingers from his clothing. Looking into her fresh young face, someone he had never seen before, why did it feel so natural for her to be here? He liked this young girl but dismissed the thought as soon as it arrived in his head but liking the way her hair lay loosely about her shoulders and her smile in her heart shaped face registered somewhere deep inside him. Then the look on his face became serious. "Next time stay nearer the lodge." Seeing again the tanned face and flash of white teeth, he waved to Angus and Mary. He was undeniably handsome and as one with his powerful horse. Drawing a deep breath, she watched his disappearing shape, thinking perhaps he was a trifle arrogant.

With a mixture of pleasure and annoyance, she walked towards the lodge thinking over the afternoon. "You are trespassing, young lady – huh – who does he think he is?" she said scanning the landscape, but he had gone. "Next time, stay nearer the lodge, Mr pompous James." But she immediately knew she didn't mean it; he had probably thought she was just a young girl…oh, well.

Now in the rose garden and breathing in there scent, she smiled to herself hearing Aunt Matty telling her – they stand for love, Helen dear. *Wait till I tell her about*...she stopped abruptly and knew this time the tears would come, stumbling to a garden bench allowed herself to let go and sobbed.

A large blue hankie swam before her eyes. "Come on, lassie, Mary's goin to make ee a nice cup o tea, and where's your shoes?" Helen blew her nose and tried to smile at him through rainbow tears then looked at her feet remembering that one sandal was where ever James had put it. The warm tingle returned.

Angus rubbed his gardener's hands together nervously; he looked around for Mary, but she had gone in, wanting her to soothe the girl's hurt. He loved the family dearly but was no good with tears; he would have cried with her. "You'll be coming to the kitchen, lassie, fer ye tea in a wee moment."

Pushing open the heavy wooden door together and looking up at the roses that hung in a low arch above it, she felt the same fierce love her aunt had known. Putting her arms around Angus then holding his hankie out to him noticed a tear on his weather-beaten face and dabbed it making them both smile. "Aunt Matty loved the rose garden."

"Aye, she did that." He turned and went towards the kitchen.

Walking slowly upstairs, she confided to her bare feet that whatever Mr James of the McKlinross land…on the beautiful horse…said, she would be going back for her sandal. Over tea and cake in the cosy kitchen, she told Mary and Angus all about the day's happenings. "Do you think you might know the gentleman?" She then waited for Angus to settle himself in his comfortable armchair next to the range.

"Aye, I think I might know." Then he picked up his mug with a wink to Mary but didn't go any further.

That evening, with closed eyes, Helen let the warm bath water relax her and sorted out in her mind what she would do tomorrow. There would be the appointment with her aunt's lawyers and lunch with the solicitor; they certainly did things differently here; she had lots of questions, knowing her aunt did own some land.

The address on one of the letters from the solicitor had puzzled her. She already knew Angus and Mary were to stay at the lodge. Their home was the roomy ground floor, as neither of them liked stairs. This pleased her as they had always been there with Aunt Matty, just like a family, although they had seemed a little surprised when Helen moved into the whole of the upstairs of the lodge a week ago. They were welcoming and said they would now be pleased to have some young company and would carry on as they did for their beloved Matty.

Sprinkling more perfumed bath salts, laying slowly back and enjoying the warm depth, found herself recalling happy memories. Her parents and two older brothers had spent almost every school holiday here until she was twelve, then just her as her brothers went on what they called adventure holidays with their friends and organisations. Helen did miss them at first.

Her father's health had been poor for a few years. Her brothers went off to college and university, but she had come at every opportunity, drawn like a magnet loving the highlands. Aunt Matty was her father's younger sister, and she fussed over them all at every opportunity. Helen and her brothers knew every path, tree and burn of the glen, and they loved every inch of it.

Breathing the steamy perfume and pressing the soft sponge under her chin, she smiled. One year, she had been allowed to join the annual shieling, to her mother's horror but her delight. Joining the mass exodus of the glen folk, cattle and all to higher grazing up in the hills below the mountains and to live in little stone huts with turf roofs that their forefathers had built. To sleep on dried heather and leaves with its heady aroma and play under the waterfalls. At night, listen to the storytelling by the old time highlanders as the taint of wood smoke hung heavily in the mist. It had been nothing less than paradise to her and the other children. Just one dark thought. The time one of the menfolk had returned with a deer he had killed, hanging it up under one of the cavernous waterfalls.

Remembering how they had been laughing and splashing when they had discovered it. Stroking the soft brown head and looking into the staring eyes, oh, how she had cried not believing it was dead. The other children were used to this side of life and told her not to be silly, but one young boy, shy, pale with dark hair had comforted her. Only going that one year, she never saw him again. Making little waves with her hands, she tried to remember his name, humming to herself, *Ross, yes, that was it, Ross*. Helen sat bolt upright spilling some of the bath water, with sudden realisation. *It couldn't be*. Of course, James McKlinross. The children of the glen only used the ends of surnames to call each other by, and James was Ross. Sliding into the soothing depth, no, he wouldn't remember her; it was too many years ago, at least ten. After all, she was Helen Glenkerry, known as Kerry. No, he wouldn't remember her.

Over the next few days, the memory of his nearness and whole being would not be shut out. It taunted her in her dreams and mingled with her food. In her quiet moments, he intruded on her innermost thoughts, sending the now familiar ripples of pleasure through her. Even finding herself scolding her reflection Helen Glenkerry get to grips with yourself.

The meeting with the solicitor had been postponed for a couple of days while he searched for some missing papers, so Helen took the opportunity to put the time to good use. Rising early and slipping on a robe, she opened her window and leaned out towards the pale rising sun. There was a fresh chill in the wind, and Helen breathed it deeply. As far as the eye could see were heather-covered slopes and hills in their first rosy flush. It was June, and by August, the heather would be purple, then last of all, flame-coloured glows before it was gone in October. That's when the stags would start to roar in the hills. Helen could see the great loch with the sea beyond and the sombre mountains looking black against the morning sky.

Today, she had decided to trace the path of the missing sandal. It had been three days now, and if she left it any longer, there was a chance she may never find it. One surprising thing she had found out, that Aunt Matty owned a vast amount of highland land and that they would be looking at the consequence of this. Also, there were tenants to meet that were, as the solicitor put it, far flung. Looking through her, as yet, few belongings and deciding on her pale blue loose-ankled jersey ski pants and top to match. Over this, she pulled a midnight blue fine wool loose sweater. The two complimented her figure and colouring. Moving to Scotland meant a change of wardrobe, and she reluctantly parted with most of her dance clothes.

Feeling the soft leather of her flat white shoes, she put them on, immediately filling her with nostalgia. Looking at herself in the long mirror, her reflection looked back at her confirming she was every inch a dancer. Her heart belonged to dance, but unfortunately, her stature had been unaware of her dreams, and she hadn't grown tall enough for same height chorus dancers but had enjoyed the dances she did get into.

Dancing for Angus and Mary brought smiles to their faces. Pantomime season was always enjoyable with her many dance friends and sharing digs. They were good times; they had laughed a lot and shared sad as well as happy times.

When her aunt had become quite frail, for some of the time she had been nursed in her Kensington apartment. Helen had been with her a lot and her dancer friends had popped in still in costume, which Aunt Matty had loved.

In one of her good periods, wanting to go back home, she died suddenly.

Helen never went back to dancing, but all her friends were still in that world. The letter had changed her life; her home was now the lovely old lodge and goodness knows how far the land stretched, but she would soon know. As neither of her brothers were interested in actually living in Scotland, they had come to an arrangement that the boys would have their parent's property in London and Matty's in Kensington, which suited them both, along with a monetary settlement to be arranged. None of them would have financial worries. It was still like an unreal happening and being in a dream state.

All this time, she had been fingering her hair, and now, it was in the familiar ballet dancer's hairstyle, swept tightly back and rolled under at the back of her head. Clipping a few wayward strands into place, she did a dainty twirl to the mirror and danced down the stairs and into the garden. Pulling the heavy door open, sunlight flooded in and for the moment, she stood under the arch of roses breathing deeply. Looking at the sky, she picked her jacket from the coat cupboard by the door. At the site of her, Angus paused from his digging and waved her over. She ran across the lawn and danced around him. Helen had done this many times over the years, making his pleasant weathered face light up and hear him chuckle. "Och, now will ye no stop still a moment, child!" His face became serious. "Now, will ye no go stray in too far on your own, lassie?"

Her shoulders drooped for a moment, then deciding to tell him all about it, they sat together on the stonewall. "So you see," she finished, "I really would like to find the other one." The old gardener smiled indulgently at her. He bent to smell a cluster of roses, caressing them as he did so. "The place you speak of is—"

"Tell you what, lassie" – she slid off the wall and stood beside him – "I have to take my Mary and her friend to the town for a wee while." She waited for him to finish clipping some roses. "When I come back, I'll walk over the rise and start to go down the glen and wait fer ee, girlie."

Opening her mouth, then closing it again, she saw the set of his chin. Angus looked proudly at the rose in his hand then tucked it into her hair. Mary joined them, and they watched her go. "Och, she's a bonny lass and no mistaking," she said smiling at her husband. Angus looked at Mary's stocky figure, rosy cheeks and wayward grey hair. Mary was a good woman, and he adored her. As she went to go back in the lodge he said, "Will ye stand still fer a minute?" He tucked a rose behind her ear.

"Angus McGregor, what'll ye be a doin to me." She tapped his arm. "Whatever will Molly Anderson think?"

"She'll think you be a lucky girl." Mary looked at the rose in his hand and took it. "Well now, that'll make two of us." She bustled in calling over her shoulder, "Now are you no goin to wash yasel before we're away, oh and did ye have a wee word about James; you should put the lass in the picture."

"Not yet, plenty oh time." Mary tut-tutted going into the lodge patting the rose behind her ear.

Angus had great affection for James McKlinross, and he had seen the way he looked at Helen Glenkerry; they made a handsome pair. He was sure young Helen was here to stay, or would she eventually want to go back to that other world of hers. He and Mary would have to wait and see.

Half running half dancing, Helen made her way to the place she had been a few days before, now feeling hot sat on a heathery outcrop with her feet resting on a boulder. Pulling her sweater carefully over her head and pushing some clips back, she laid it across her shoulders. Taking the small silver binoculars from her pocket, she sat looking at the delicate tracery of swirls, remembering them as a child in a velvet purse her aunt always carried. Sighing, she forced herself to concentrate on finding her sandal.

Looking through the lenses, she found herself following the contours of the mountains, dark and rising steeply. So steeply in fact the heather had failed to live on it. The distant view was sombre, greying, as Helen scanned slowly thinking it seemed to have a scowl today. The wind was a little chill now. Watching the sea birds circling above the gorge, she thought they might be eagles. Looking about her, she wasn't at all sure that this was the way she came before. Pinpointing the lock, it seemed to go into infinity. Scanning left, she could see the castle on the shoreline. Studying it more closely, she made out the battlements, tower and four turrets. It made a truly bold picture; her aunt had called it a symphony in stone.

Glimpsing a wood of sycamore trees beyond the castle and noticing the rapid change in vegetation, pine, oak, fern then the ground changed to grassy slopes, and away in the distance, Helen knew were the spectacular Kinray Falls. The breeze was colder now and tugged at her secured hair. Taking one more quick look at the castle, she could see that it protruded into the water, surrounded by a velvet carpet of moss grass. Its sheer beauty brought an involuntary sigh, the vast loch, the dense forest, becoming sparse then just grassy slopes into the hills.

Helen knew that somewhere along the mountain face was an almost undetectable fissure through which you could take a boat into the open sea, the Atlantic Ocean, its outer coastline giving no clue to the hidden sanctuary of the loch beyond its granite exterior. Helen shivered and trained the glasses back on the burn, as she scanned along the bank, a dark mass filled the lens. Slowly lowering the glasses, she watched James McKlinross ride up to her. For a moment, panic filled her, then she laughed inwardly at herself. Knowing she had every right to be here and sure he hadn't recognised her. Standing up quickly as the horse turned its head to look at her, the large intelligent eyes reflecting her image, then it lowered its head pulling the grasses at her feet.

Looking up at him, she saw him smile. When he spoke, his voice was almost stern. "What have you done to your hair?" Suddenly remembering her appearance, she looked away. "You look like" – she looked sharply back at him; had he recognised her; she waited – "…like someone from Swan Lake." Not unkindly, but his words made her wince inwardly. He wasn't to know their significance. If he had, they would never have passed his lips. He would never knowingly hurt this lovely girl standing below him. In the recesses of his mind, there seemed to be an awareness, a stirring as he gazed at her, mixed with tingling pleasure; she was not a young girl; she was a woman, and he intended to get to know her better. He felt there was a gentle vulnerability about her in spite of the tilt of her chin. Helen turned and walked away.

Feeling slightly irritated, picking her sweater up from the boulder where she had let it drop, she fastened it around her waist. Not wanting to look for her sandal in his presence. Taking one last look through her binoculars, she noticed he also was. "I suppose you are looking for trespasses." It sounded almost rude.

She saw him stiffen, but he let the remark go. "I'm glad to see you wearing shoes; if you knew more about the terrain of the highlands, you wouldn't take risks."

Helen felt the niggle again, he sounded almost pompous. Raising the glasses and twisting slightly in the saddle, 'yes, I've been riding the boundaries'. Helen felt like laughing but controlled the moment, smiling to herself as she lowered the glasses. 'I shall be looking at boundaries myself', 'when', 'soon' 'where exactly'. Slipping the little silver binoculars into her pocket and smoothing the bulge, she unfastened her sweater from around her waist and pulled it over her head unwittingly loosening her hair letting the rose fall to the ground unnoticed.

"Where exactly?" he persisted. His expression had changed to puzzlement. James had dismounted, but Helen had already started to pick her way along the stony path. Without looking around, she shrugged her shoulders.

"On a map."

He walked to where the rose lay and deftly picked it up, tucking it into the pocket next to his heart. In a few strides, he had caught Helen up. Walking back, they chatted comfortably, in between James stopping to survey the landscape; soon the lodge was in sight, and Angus could be seen coming over the ridge. James touched her arm; they had stopped. Looking at each other, he seemed nervous. "Would you let me take you out?" He was thinking about his favourite place, high in the hills and onto an outcrop that seemed to be suspended in space with breath-taking vistas. Helen's eyes were wide with surprise as a pleasurable feeling filled her; she wanted to blurt out 'yes, yes, yes'. Glancing in the direction Angus was coming in, James waited, then heard himself say, "Perhaps another time then." Helen gave him a wide smile and gracefully accepted the offer.

"Thank you, I would like that very much," she said noting the relieved expression. He ran his fingers through his hair pushing the dark waves that curled between his fingers, off his forehead and smiled, a flash of white in a tanned face. With one movement, he was astride his horse. "I'll call at the lodge to see you; we can make arrangements then."

His heart was soaring; this beautiful creature had agreed to let him take her out. There was something he had to do first. As they were almost to Angus, he rode forward and spoke to him. Helen caught a little of their conversation. "Well, laddie, as long as I know mind, I dinna object." Helen watched the two men part with a handshake.

Angus and Helen walked the last few yards over the ridge and into the rose garden. The wind was getting stronger making the flowers sway about. Putting her hand to her hair she said, "Oh, Angus, my flower's gone."

"Dinna fret, there's plenty more – at least, you've still got your shoes on." They were both laughing as they went their separate ways at the bottom of the wide stairway. Helen hesitated. "Angus." He smiled to himself hearing the question in her voice and answered before she asked.

"He comes from way across the glen." Turning to look at her flushed cheeks and shining eyes he said, "I reckon you'll be seeing a might more oh the lad if I'm any judge." Not for the first time that day, Helen blushed; she ran up the stairs.

"Angus McGregor, what can you be thinking of?" She sounded just like his Mary he mused, and toying with his thoughts, Angus McGregor was thinking of plenty.

As things stood, he told himself, fate didn't need him to interfere; she was allowing things to go along very nicely, to his mind, thank you.

The faint aroma of Mary's cooking had immediately whetted her appetite, realising she was suddenly very hungry. Now unfolding the embroidered napkin, she closed her eyes and said a quick thank you for this wonderful food Mary had put before her. A salmon steak, no doubt from the loch, garnished with sprigs of dill, buttered potatoes sat in a terrine. Mary's famous mustard sauce was in a jug, golden whipped and fluffy. Five tempting strawberries looked at her from a glass dish. Angus's pride and joy. She ate with relish. The casement doors stood wide open framed by patterned woven curtains, giving a view of lowlands, glens and mountains. After such a meal, Helen sat for a while losing herself dreamily in the view and was suddenly aware of Mary putting coffee in front of her. Helen put the dishes on the tray while Mary poured, then ventured, 'Where does James come from?' Mary looked at the open doors.

"Och, way across the glen by the lake." Sipping her coffee, she looked into Mary's rosy face and smiled patiently.

"Yes, but where across the glen exactly?" Mary stopped and folded her hands across her apron and looked straight at the girl.

"Why, it's the castle of course." Her voice held traces of surprise. Picking up the tray, she nodded to the dresser. "Don't go forgetting your post, lass." And deftly closed the door.

Helen was thoughtful. So, he was in the employ of the castle; she had been right then about the crest on his saddle blanket. Picking up her post, she read the message from the Balentines, the American couple in the Big House along the drive.

Taking the stairs two at a time, she was soon curled up in the cushions of her armchair. The invitation to visit David and Lucinda Balantine, mentioning they would like to discuss their tenancy with her and the forthcoming ball, which they hoped to gain her approval. This sounded exciting and what a lovely idea; she was eager to see inside the house too.

Opening the long white envelope with the words 'Royal Hotel' on the headed notepaper made her laugh. It was clearly Claudette's handwriting, and unfolding the several sheets, she smiled knowing it would transport her back to that magical world of dance, her great love. She was already laughing softly to herself. "Jo Jo's massaging my feet, so if the writing goes a bit skew whiff you'll know the reason; he doesn't change, Helen; everyone sends their love. We've just finished at the Royal Theatre after five months; technically, we're all out of a job, still, the auditions will come along soon, and it will all start again.

"Last Wednesday, Fran mislaid a pink ballet shoe. I had visions of her hopping through the adagio. Tito came to the rescue. I don't think anyone noticed one was white…" Helen could imagine the scene back stage. "Anyway, how's Scotland treating you, have you managed to get the things sorted that were worrying you? We were all saying, wouldn't it be great if we could get a stint in Edinburgh; we could all descend on you. (You are near Edinburgh, aren't you…?) Guess what, we had some workman come in to mend the stage floor, supposed to be putting a sprung floor in, well, some of the male dancers were exercising. Taking the mickey was a bad mistake, seven years training in dance to jump the heights they do…We did some patching up (and some cover up grease paint), and they ended up shaking hands. I'm sure these burly workman had a change of mind about male dancers. Archie on the theatre door says to be remembered to you; he's moving to the Apollo, that will be a loss for the Royal, what he doesn't know isn't worth knowing, oh and Jacky and Mark are walking out, who knows, it might be a big hat job, Helen. Well, bye for now, don't do anything I wouldn't do that's giving you a lot of rope, darling. Love you lots. Claudette XX"

Sighing and slowly getting ready for bed, her thoughts were of all her friends; she would have liked to be there with them, just for a few hours, knowing it to be impossible at the moment. Deciding tomorrow, she would get her sketchbook out and try to get Cavalier drawn, but for now, she had a letter to write.

Chapter 2

It was unusually mild today. Angus had brought out the wooden loungers with the flowery comfy cushions, and Helen was now gratefully relaxing, after feeling pleased with her sketch of James's horse Cavalier.

Stretching lazily, enjoying the warmth the sheltered corner afforded her and closing her eyes, she remembered her privileged ride home on him a few days ago bringing back the goosebumps once again. Lifting the sketch and shading her eyes, she looked at it more closely; yes, she was sure she had caught a good likeness of him.

Feeling her eyes closing again, she allowed the comfort and warmth to let her drift into sleep. The sound of a car door closing a little while later woke her, but she was reluctant to move.

Opening her eyes, she suddenly realised it was James McKlinross, and he was coming in her direction. Now, she wished fervently she had paid more attention to dressing this morning and looked at her flimsy attire with mounting irritation. As his footsteps came closer, she lay back picking up one of the cushions and watched his approach. As he saw her, his smile broadened causing the sun to glint momentarily on white teeth, his dark hair shining in the morning sun. Helen pushed her hair back off her forehead and waited.

Unable to take her eyes from him, she was hypnotised by the strong lithe legs, his easy stride eating up the space between them. Her heartbeat quickened. Had he noticed the surprised pleasure at his unexpected appearance. A brief annoyance at herself, she lowered her eyes as his polished riding boots came into focus.

Unprepared as she was for visitors, especially this man who set her cheeks flaming and heart to miss a beat, causing her unable to finish her intended words. Discreetly pulling the flimsy satin top a little firmer around her, she waited.

The sketchpad resting on her knees with her drawing of Cavalier suddenly registered. Hurriedly closing its stiff cover, Helen picked up one of the cushions, as his shadow fell across her, immobilising her movements for the moment.

Glancing at the pencil being twisted nervously, 'busy'. In one swift appraisal, he saw the heart-shaped face already starting to colour and how her hair framed her face with the early sun highlighting her hair. Her eyes were still lowered making her long lashes more noticeable. A telltale quiver at the corner of his lips belying an effort not to smile, knowing well the effect his presence was having on the skimpily clad Helen.

Making a decision and swinging her legs neatly from the lounger into a sitting position didn't make much improvement to her predicament. Glaringly aware of her clothes, she was still reluctant to stand up. Now having control of her breathing, she raised her head and looked into his handsome face and clear eyes, just as he broke into a breath-taking smile.

An immediate feeling of defeat, as the sight of this man brought back long ago memories. Such happy times when they were children. She could almost hear and feel the waterfall.

Smiling, 'to what do I owe this visit', managing a cool tone and returning his smile, pulling the finger-length robe a little tighter. "I've come to see Angus, I've brought his car back," he said giving the keys a little toss.

Slightly annoyed with herself and indicating towards the lodge house she said, "I think Angus is in the kitchen." She hoped she would have a moment to put something more fitting on.

When he made no attempt to go towards the kitchen, she tried again, "Would you like to see if Angus is…" He moved closer.

"No, that's okay. Am I interrupting?" he asked nodding to the sketchbook while taking in the slim ankles and graceful legs, appreciating how the silk top lay outlining her firm breasts, the sash around her slim waist, the soft folds resting on the curve of her hips and upper thighs.

Reigning in his thoughts. "I would very much like a cold drink."

Seizing the opportunity, Helen said, "Good idea, so would I…why don't you ask Mary, while I…"

"Certainly." He turned and went into the house. Looking at his receding back, this man puzzled her. Taking the stairs two at a time and in her room, she pulled on blue cotton trousers and her Spanish blouse. Pushing her feet into her silver sandals and feeling a lot more comfortable, she skipped back down the stairs to find Mary, Angus and James, comfortably seated around the garden table, sipping squash. James pulled a chair out for her, next to him and slid her drink towards her.

Angus looked at Helen appreciatively; the scoop neck Spanish blouse was very becoming. He put his glass down, noting James's expression with satisfaction. "Lovely, don't you think so, James?" he asked picking up his glass again. "Mary's homemade lemonade." James coughed.

"The lemonade. Yes" – a slight pause – "among other things," he said looking at Helen. Mary was smiling.

"Helen always looks lovely but did you like my homemade drink?"

"Lovely."

James passed Angus's car keys to him. "Thanks, lad. Helen has an appointment with the solicitor in the morning; I think tomorrow will be a busy day. We will have quite a few maps to study, and I know he's very keen on the demarcation line. Nice chap the solicitor, very helpful."

James digested the information; he had been hoping to take Helen out tomorrow, but learning she had an appointment, he would have to wait a little bit longer. In his mind, he had been planning a picnic. Leaning towards Helen, James looked directly into Helen's eyes. "So these are the maps you were referring to yesterday?" Taken a little by surprise, she shrugged her shoulders.

"It's so nice today; let's not talk about stuffy things." She finished her drink. "You'll have to show me how to make this, Mary."

"You made this with me when you were a wee girl, knee high to a grass hopper."

Chapter 3

Helen sat in the large office. Noises of the bustling town wafted through the window like an insistent rhythm. The solicitor stood at her elbow. Mr Bloomfield's voice was kindly. "I didn't realise you weren't in full possession of the facts." Her hand shook as she sipped at the glass offered to her. "I'm so sorry I had to break our lunch date; it was unavoidable, I'm afraid."

The solicitor returned to his side of the desk. "Are there any questions you would like to ask, my dear?" Looking at her for a moment he said, "I have a typescript here with everything you need to know about your inheritance; I'm afraid it carries a hefty death duty sum. It's set out fully." He shuffled some papers.

This feeling of everything not being quite real came again. The thought she had been dreaming and would wake up at any moment. Putting the glass down she took the shaft of papers held out to her. "It has come as a bit of a shock; I really didn't know." Looking across at Angus and Mary, she attempted to explain why the sudden knowledge of the Big House was now also hers.

Big House, it was in fact the most beautiful stone Scottish mansion boasting one hundred rooms. Helen had admired it many times from a distance. "You see, Aunt Matty never mentioned she owned" – her eyes lowered to the old black and white photo attached to the papers – "this part of the estate. I've only ever known her live in the." Helen smoothed her skirt down. "No wonder you were a little surprised when I moved into the lodge with you." She smiled apologetically over her shoulder.

Mary got up and came over, putting a reassuring hand on her arm. "Och, look, child, as far as we're concerned, you carry on living at the lodge if that's what you want, lassie; it's far too large for us wee two." Mary straightened up and beamed at Mr Bloomfield who had been watching them with a knowledgeable eye. He had always thought a lot of Angus and Mary having handled Matty's affairs for many years.

Mary looked at Angus. "We always promised Matty we would never be far away from the wee girl, why, she was born in the lodge, oh, the excitement after two boys. Angus knows all about the running of the estate; he's no a young man, but he'll do his best." Patting Helen's shoulder, she sat down.

Angus smiled indulgently at her. It went without saying they would look after Helen just like they looked after Matty. "Until you tell me otherwise, lassie." Helen got up and kissed them both on the cheek feeling grateful to them all; she knew she was going to need all the help she could get and trusted these knowledgeable people.

The solicitor gave Angus some old maps of the estate and said he would go over the boundaries with him if he was unsure of any demarcation lines but that it was quite straightforward. He made another appointment for a month's time in case any difficulties would arise by then.

Helen wondered briefly what James would make of this. Shaking hands warmly, Helen knew things would never be quite the same again. A new life beckoned to her; she would have great responsibilities, and a very different girl stepped into the street, from two hours ago.

"The bank is this way, Helen." Angus ushered her along the busy street. Helen looked at her watch.

"We don't have to hurry; I've got another thirty minutes to my appointment." She smiled at him. "Angus, 1 think I'd like to spend the rest of the day in town."

"Just as you please, lass. Dinna ye forget the Balentines, 7.30 pm." Then with a boyish grin, he added, "At your place." He pushed the oak and glass door for her and watched as she walked into the cool interior of the bank.

Sitting down to lunch at their favourite eating place, Angus confided, "You know, the future is going to be very interesting, Mary; I'm sure our part of the highlands is in good hands. Did you manage to get all the things you wanted, I saw you making for the bairns shop." She looked out of the window and touched the back of his rough hand. "I canna help thinking Helen's in for another shock."

"Aye, but a pleasant one. Matty didna care for the affairs of money."

"Angus, you know, it'll take a bit of time for her to get used to;   the estate is vast."

"Don't go worrying yer bonny head about that now, worry about the menu." "Did I tell you Molly said Mrs McKlinross wants us to visit her and is looking forward to meeting Helen?"

Angus smiled "Did she now."

"Mmmm, it'll be nice for Helen to see the castle and a bit of the McKlinross estate. Molly says the boys are quite excited as James has another champion in the making, this one has come on right out of the blue, and that's what his name is 'Out of the Blue'. Isn't that good?" Angus was thoughtful.

"That must be the one Stuart was talking about out of 'Lady of the Loch'. Och, there's nothing like the highland cattle and good old Aberdeen, Angus." He smiled to himself.

"There's nothing like starting at the deep end, as they say, Mary. Balantines tonight then castle soon; we mustna rush her." Mary caught the twinkle in Angus's eye; she wasn't really sure why it was there but was content to see it there anyway. Angus spread his napkin and thought about the castle. Their starter arrived, cream of vegetable soup. Chunks of fresh tasty vegetables. "How is Andrew getting on now that he and Ginty live in the castle, the new bairn is due in two months."

"Molly says all's fine; it must make things a bit easier with the two brothers and their cousin sharing the work load and worry."

A frown crossed Angus's brow. "It's the rustling that is their biggest worry, those laddies are gonna have to get to the bottom of that before too long." He sighed and his frown deepened and his eyes held that far off look. Mary new what he was thinking. She stroked the back of his hand.

"It's no good going back over the past." Angus sighed.

"It was a cruel blow; their father's accident; they were only laddies. He was a great man and a good friend. Ah, Mary, I miss him to this day." Mary let him speak. He needed to air the thoughts that set him brooding.

Mary's face suddenly beamed. "I'll tell you something that will cheer you up; our Helen says she's going to get a new image." Angus was all ears now.

"She doesn't need a new what kind of image deye mean, woman?"

"Oh, Angus. A new hairstyle. She's going to get her hair cut and altered." Her eyes twinkled at him with her secret. "Aye and did ye know she's going to look at cars." They were both smiling broadly, as their steaming Scottish stew arrived.

Stepping into the inn, the change in light made Helen blink. Choosing a carved bench seat with velvet cushions by the window, she put her parcels alongside her. Toying with the idea of slipping her shoes off under the table, she studied her surroundings. The inn was fairly crowded; looking at her watch, she decided she could relax for half an hour, before the man from the garage would be turning up, then home.

Feeling the strangeness of her shorter shoulder-length hair, she sipped the cool drink. At first, she had been alarmed at the amount of hair on the salon floor, but the mirror confirmed she still possessed quite an amount. It had been expertly shaped and now lay obediently on her shoulders, framing her face. Looking out of the window, she would be able to see her new car arrive from this vantage point.

Sitting back, she noted the different characters around her, lilting and strong dialect, mix of local and visitors alike. Above where she sat hung two pictures, one of a castle with round turrets and a fairytale look and the other was morning light across the loch.

The conversation of the three men directly behind her was becoming heated, with accents so broad she could only grasp snippets of their conversation in course harsh whispers.

"He's a big brute."

"Aye, take some shiftin."

"You sure you can get the wheels. Canna be no moon."

"I seen im."

"When?"

"When I delivered the feed." Then the conversation turned to low mumbling, but a few names were audible. "Got choice Lakeland Lover." More mumbling and what sounded like the word blue and lady – something loch. Helen tried to concentrate on what she would wear tonight but listened.

A wine-coloured Rover drew up silently outside the window, and Helen felt a flush of delight. She hurriedly collected her parcels. Making her way to the door, she bumped shoulders with an unsavoury looking man. His unshaven face leered at her, and she was acutely aware of strong body odour and stale whiskey.

Now she sat in the plush upholstery of her new car being chauffeur driven home by the man from the garage. The bank manager's advice had been sound, and she had taken it. Yes, now she had a position to keep up and reliable transport if she wanted to reach her tenants and the hill farmers, so she had also ordered a Land Rover to be delivered in three weeks' time. Breathless at the figures mounting up but she wasn't going to worry about the money, the bank manager had already done a rough estimate, and it had hardly scratched the surface. Helen seriously began to wonder where all her aunt's wealth had come from.

Later, she had waved Aunt Matty's old car goodbye. The garage hand had promised to find it a deserving home. "Dinna you fret non, I'll see she goes to a good home." Dear Angus would not be parted from his old car.

Leaving Angus inspecting the new car with a broad grin and Mary sitting in the front seat making lots of oohs and aahs and saying her feet didn't touch the floor, Helen went and changed for the Balentines. She had decided to walk the drive up to the Big House and give herself time to think. There was a lot going on in her head. Little things Angus and Mary had said were now beginning to make sense. No doubt, the Balentines were eager to discuss their tenancy, a fact she hadn't been aware of before. She hoped fervently they would be there for a very long time.

Chapter 4

Looking at the outline of the Big House standing majestically on the side of the hill sheltered from the north wind, Helen was suddenly filled with fear. Whispering under her breath Aunt Matty help. How am I going to manage something so grand? With the last rays of the setting sun dropping behind the hill, the house looked bathed in pale gold with red to one side. Stopping to take in the view, she could just make out a rough terrain Land Rover pulling up to the house.

Twenty minutes later, Helen was walking slowly up the stone steps as she slowly surveyed her aunt's old ancestral home. There were elegant seats and ornamental urns decked the ancient flagstones. At the top of the steps were impressive large statues on either side of her of magnificent stags. Calmly soaking up the atmosphere around her, she turned and stood between the two stags, and like them, she stared across the glen, only her thoughts were of living flesh and blood, wondering where out there was 'he' tonight.

Although Helen had not quite reached the door, it opened quietly as she turned around. The maid smiled at the look on Helen's face, her surprise had been obvious. She hadn't expected the maid to be dressed in pastel pink. A tiny white apron adorned her waist and an arch of white pleats across her head. Entering into the rich atmosphere, she was again surprised, her feet sunk into deep carpet. A chandelier hung from a high centre point, the crystal droplets sparkling like thousand jewels. Everywhere pervaded an air of elegant richness and graceful comfort. Ahead was a curving staircase with long pictures all the way up. Helen had a vision of all the ladies that had made an entrance down that staircase in their gowns over the years. Feeling a hand on her elbow, she obediently followed the maid. Everything seemed larger than life, even the huge doors she was being shown through, just having time to glimpse the picture on either side.

One of a Scottish Piper in the Glenkerry tartan and the other bore the ornate coat of arms on a shield over crossed swords. The maid knocked and entered. Helen followed, liking immediately the middle-aged woman that greeted her. "Helen, come in. Lucinder Balentine." She held out her slim hand. Demurely elegant with coiffured hair, her lilac dress hanging tastefully about her hips. "David will join us in a few minutes; he has someone with him at the moment. Now, let us get acquainted." She handed her a cut glass goblet. "David's pride and joy, after his prize cattle of course, so I'm afraid the first drink is compulsory." Helen took a small sip, then a bigger sip; it was very pleasant.

"Where does he grow his grapes because this is good." Not that Helen new that much about wine.

"He will be pleased. The greenhouses have been specially adapted to keep them happy in our climate," Lucinder replied as she refilled their drinks.

Voices could be heard and the door opened as David Balantine strode in. "Yes, that's just what we need. Come in, James and meet our new neighbour." Helen suddenly felt hot as James came over and shook her hand also putting his other hand on top. Then they both laughed, and he held her hand for some time.

"Yes, we have met at the lodge; in fact, I'm hoping to take Helen to see some of the beauty spots." She felt him squeeze her hand then he reluctantly let it go. The next hour passed pleasantly, but Helen was getting nervous; she didn't want anything to come up in the conversation and have him learn about her situation until she had put him in the picture herself.

Helen blinked; David was speaking to her. "My bulls, I want you to see my bulls." And with that, she was escorted into another room full of pictures of cattle.

James whispered to her, "Eight tomorrow morning – picnic." Then he took his leave from the Balantines. He could already see Angus waiting outside with his old runabout, not wanting Helen to do the dusty walk back.

"I'm relieved to know you are happy with our tenancy, being American in Scotland, one is never quite sure of local feeling," They smiled at each other. "But I feel we are already beginning a great friendship, and you are happy about the ball, oh, it's fun, isn't it?"

Helen climbed into Angus's old car with a yawn, grateful the conversations hadn't got out of hand, telling Angus and Mary how the evening went and about the bulls and the wine. "David gave us a bottle of his wine; we must get around to drinking it, Angus. Mary, you will both love it. I'm taking my supper to bed;

it appears I'm going on a picnic tomorrow so I'll have to be up early." Helen noticed the smile that passed between them.

Rising early, she showered. Slipping a robe on, she opened her windows as wide as they would go and leaned towards the rising sun. Just knowing James was out there somewhere gave her heart a lift. The breeze had a chill, but she knew it wouldn't bother her. Now what would be suitable for a picnic, feeling a ripple of excitement she opened her wardrobe. Soon she would be sitting next to James in the Land Rover and a delicious picnic to look forward to. Dear Mary had handed her a wicker basket just as James arrived. Soon they were headed for the hills.

Holding his hand out, he stopped and looked at her. "Helen, you look lovely." She blushed at the sudden unexpected compliment and smiled as he helped her into the Land Rover.

Angus waved them off. "Take care, lad, you've got precious cargo there."

James looked over his shoulder. "My thoughts exactly, Angus. I'll take good care of her."

Today, she felt so happy; her heart was bursting just to be near him. They had left the Land Rover a little way down the valley and were now winding their way along a sheep track when he began to tell her about their surroundings. Helen hung on his every word; she marvelled at the information laid before her. His voice was so good to listen to; it reminded her of the storytelling in the shieling days. "There are multitudes of basalt dykes, did you know we have some ancient volcanos," seeing her stop, added, "only small ones, but the glen folk do tell of plates that rattle on a windless night." Smiling, his fingers resting lightly on her shoulder, she felt a gentle pressure. The scent of clover and birdsong made her feel heady.

As they started to climb the rocky slopes, the vegetation altered. His hand brushed her arm, then his touch was gone. Helen slowed and studied him. His effortless strides, the strong shoulders, she smiled to herself, volcanos indeed. As if he had heard her thoughts, turning to look at her just below him, he said, "Just the odd tremor," and held out his hand for her. She knew only too well the – odd tremor. Helen was beginning to experience them with increasing regularity.

They had stopped for a moment to drink. "When our family used to come to the lodge, in the evening Aunt Matty used to tell my brothers and me about her memories as a child, when her mother and father went with the shieling folk and the animals to higher pastures for the summer; she always said they were the happiest times of her childhood. Although it was hard for the grownups, for the children, all being together was bliss." Then unthinking she added, "That's why she encouraged us to…" She had been going to say, 'encouraged us to go with the shieling that one summer, knowing we would come back happy and healthy'. Deciding to continue her aunt's memories. "They would 34 pass through villages, and people and their animals would join them adding to the throng on the move." James now lay stretched out on the grass toying with a wisp of seeding grass, his memory unfolding. They were both quiet now for some time, then Helen remembered something else, raising herself on her elbow she said, "Do you know" – the remark brought a smile to his face – "the women had to carry everything they needed for the long stay on their backs?"

"Mmm, in creels, that's what they were called, creels loaded with all their possessions, and some of them knitted for their menfolk as they walked along barefoot. You see, Helen, my parents and grandparents were storytellers too." Then he smiled at her astonished expression. Sighing he added, "My brother and I loved listening about the old history."

He lay back lost in thought. Helen lay back stretching lazily and closing her eyes. The fresh air was intoxicating. James turned slightly towards her; his voice was deep with feeling. "Can you imagine what it must have been like to move with the shieling?" Actually, yes, she could. A fleeting stab of disappointment passed through her once again; she wanted to shout, 'I was there with you, don't you remember me?'. Feeling her throat tighten, blinking up at the sun, she sat up. She saw James take a deep breath and say almost to himself, "It was a long time ago now, but I remember, just the once, it was pure heaven to me. It's something I'll always remember." Helen trembled.

She struggled to keep her voice calm. "Of course, the main aim was fresh pasture for the animals, and they had to be milked, the butter and crowdie made." A crystal clear picture of him teaching her to milk, their heads together, then stirring the crowdie together while she told him about her ballet classes. She was desperately trying to push out unwanted thoughts, but now, they came crowding in on her…Did he remember? Had she altered that much? Supposing she must have. Dance school certainly had changed her. Stealing a look at James, he was lying still and relaxed, eyes closed, light dappling his face and clothes. No, she was sure he didn't connect her with childhood. Knowing again that stab of sadness.

How could she broach the subject without being tactless, and that wasn't all, she had wanted to discuss the Big House with him. Not at all sure that he wasn't under the impression that she was Mary and Angus's relation. The feeling was beginning to worry her. An involuntary sigh escaped her; James sat up, leaning over her. "Come with me to the old shieling country; I'd like you to see it."

Smiling uncertainly she asked, "When?" There was a boyish excitement in his eyes.

"Now…please."

He jumped up holding his hands out to her. "It's still early, come." It was almost like a command. "There's now a good road nearly all the way." His breathing was quick and his eyes shining. Putting her hand in his, Helen heard a distinct warning voice within her.

"Come, I'll show you the ancient water line before the level of the lake dropped. It's quite unbelievable. It's on our way."

Chapter 5

Walking briskly, Helen was hardly able to keep up with him. Smiling, he asked if she was hungry, and she confirmed she was, remembering Mary's contribution to the picnic. They had reached the Land Rover, and James was looking thoughtful. "We'll eat soon; overlooking the lake, you can see the old shoreline." A few minutes later, they had turned off the road onto rough ground, and suddenly, a vista opened up that took her breath away. Now, contentedly fed, they were making their way to a mass of overhanging dark trees. He was standing a little way from her after showing her the original shoreline. To her, it had looked like a protruding lip, snaking around the hillside. There was a strange darkness, as above them great arches of twisted roots massed. He was looking across at her as she stood under the shadowy ledge.

Holding her hands up she said, "You mean a few thousand years ago, standing here I might have been drowning." His expression changed, and he pulled her firmly from the hollow.

Helen had the feeling he was going to say something, instead, he said simply, "Ten thousand actually." The place still had the faint smell of decay, the scar of another era before the level of the lake fell. It was far below them now. They walked for a while, the path was becoming difficult, and Helen found herself dislodging stones that rolled down the side of the path at alarming speed. James smiled and took a few paces towards her, stretching out his hand and pulling her onto a flat bank. He saw the back of her hand had a nasty scratch and her nail was broken. Helen was a little breathless and lent against the boulder. His gaze travelled down to her grazed hand, as if without thinking he lifted her fingers to his lips. She closed her eyes tightly and held on to the moment, his lips were soft and warm, and for one wild moment, she longed for his arms about her.

Was it the crystal air at this altitude that made her lose all perspective? James lowered her hand to rest on the boulder next to his; she watched as he lovingly passed his hand over the surface feeling the deep love he had for this land. For a fleeting moment, she envied the boulder. He was looking at her quizzically; she felt herself blush and brushed her hand across them. A slow smile lifted his mouth and there was a roughish glint in his eyes. Helen felt sure he had read her thoughts and leaned against the boulder to steady herself.

They started back, and Helen decided to ask him about some of the customs she had been reading about. He seemed lost in thought. Looking at him so characteristic of his race, and visualising him, as his Viking ancestors must have been centuries before. Helen shuddered looking quickly away from his dark masculinity. A striking likeness to the pictures in the book she had been reading. Descriptive chapters of their marauding, pillage and rape. It might have been a very different story if she had met him by the burn then.

Helen fixed her eyes on the distant purple hills. "I was reading a very interesting book," she said without looking at him, "about some of the old customs of these parts."

"And what were you reading about?" She thought for a moment.

"I was just up to The Hill Walkers, and er, The Barring Stick, a very old custom apparently." She shrugged her shoulders at him. "That's when I must have fallen asleep." He bent and picked up a stick.

"The barring stick is a very old custom, many a traveller has found an open door and been welcomed in." Helen felt a warm glow pass through her. He was looking at her strangely. "The custom was, never to close the house door during the day, summer or winter." Helen was thinking as he studied her. It was a charming custom, but she could see it did have its drawbacks. For instance, work was hard and dusty and facilities primitive, what if…She looked at James; he read the question in her expression, his voice was even.

"If for instance, the woman wanted to change her dress, or there was very little food available to share with the visitor, she would not shut the door but temporarily use the barring stick." They had stopped. Listening to his voice and watching his strong fingers, fascinated as he peeled the stick, she waited, urging him to tell her more. As they looked directly at each other, James seemed to have a strange light in his eyes. Holding out the stick to her, she took it without looking away. "For example, if you were my woman, when I was home, you would need to place the barring stick across the threshold of our house." Smiling nervously, she lowered her gaze to the stony path turning the stick slowly over. He was drawing her like a magnet to him.

Looking at him now, she took in every detail; he was standing feet slightly apart, his strength showing, arms by his sides, but she could see the whiteness of his knuckles, hands clenched in self-restraint. Should she be afraid of this man? Her eyes were now level with his broad shoulders, hesitated at the dark cleft of his neck tanned against the whiteness of his shirt. Weakness ebbed at her. Now, looking fully into his handsome face and clear wide set eyes, gripping the stick tightly, try as she might, words would not come. Neither of them moved. Helen new his eyes were making love to her, and she was responding as deep as the lake below them.

James was becoming pleasantly disturbed by her closeness. The beauty around them matched her loveliness. He had never compared his lands with a woman before. Her eyes perceived and a heart that enjoyed. He felt akin to her; she was a delight to be with.

Studying his profile now, as he drove along the hill road, she found his expression unreadable. Suddenly, her heart leapt up at her as the familiar shieling country she remembered came into view. The road they had been following turned into a single track over the hills and stretched ahead gradually opening out into the Shining country. They were both held in awe, each not knowing what the other felt. James touched her arm. "It's like we've left the world behind." Turning towards him, she wanted to blurt out, 'I know this country; I've been here before with you.' Her heart wanted to cry out, 'don't you remember?'. James sensed her looking at him and smiled as the Land Rover bumped and rocked to a stop. He lent back in his seat taking exaggerated deep breaths. "Can't you feel there's something different about the air up here?" She looked away and nodded.

He looked so relaxed. James slung the plaid rug across his shoulder and took her hand as they started to walk. Her own feelings were in turmoil. Walking alongside him, she recognised each little part. Locked away in her memory all these years. There were the remains of the little cleits, earth roofs now fallen in and scattered stones. It made her sad. Helen had to admit to herself she hadn't been prepared for the neglect of time. Looking at what was left of the little huts, dotted around the grassy slopes, she had the same feeling. They reminded her of limpets clinging to rocks. Still she walked on alongside James. He stopped, head erect, looking alert. Memories unfolding, Helen knew they had stood like this before, together on this very spot; she could see them so plainly. James looked at her; yes, she could hear it too, the unmistakable slow vibrating rumbling and knew they were near the waterfall. This had been their favourite place with all the other children.

Helen watched James spread the tartan rug and wondered if the stepping-stones were still across the lower falls. They were looking at the water gliding over the square stones above her in a silken sheet, milky bubbles teasing memories from her as they danced in the cascading water. Standing with her back to the falls, she felt its mist and spray, and her spirits soared. Oh, happy days. Just for a moment, she longed to be a child again, then a tear slowly made its way down her cheek, and she stood so the spray disguised it. As the cold waters dropped onto her upturned face, a poem swam in her memory.

'How Sweet the Taste of Momentary Bliss,

Of Careless Childhood,

The Joy of Youth in Spring,

When Youth Is Innocence.'

Shaking her damp hair back from her shoulders in an effort to dispel the old magic she slipped her shoes off and sat on the old grey familiar stone, gently lowering her dusty feet into the icy water. The memories were tumbling from her like the water over the rocks above. She had sat here that summer. Looking across at him now, standing with his back to her consumed in his own memories, he looked boyish. There had seemed something sad, and she had felt protective towards him. But she knew the reason now. Looking at the dark inner cave of the waterfall, she remembered how he had comforted her when they had found the deer hanging there. He hadn't laughed like some of the other children; he had dried her tears and comforted her.

Calling to him and patting the stone beside her she said, "Come and sit here beside me, Ross." Dipping her hands into the water, she dabbed her face. It felt just as good as it did in the shieling days. The sight, the sounds, the smell it was just the same as her childhood memories. The waterfall down the mountainside, strewn with boulders holding the pools of water they had swum in. Helen could almost hear the children's laughter, echoing. She shivered involuntary, then realised James was standing right behind her.

He was staring wide eyed at her; the hairs on the back of his neck prickled, his memory spinning back. He stood unbelieving, a ghost from the past. Nobody had called him Ross, only that one summer, his memory peeling back.

Oh why oh why did I make that mistake; she snatched her feet from the water and biting her bottom lip hard, turned away; she closed her eyes and waited, was he going to use the same tone as their first meeting by the burn. He slipped his arms gently around her damp body drawing her close to him. Breathing a sigh of relief, she relaxed against his warm body, feeling him bury his face in her hair and then kiss her ear, his voice hardly a whisper. "Kerry, Kerry." It was so wonderful to hear him use her name, just like all those years ago. "Kerry, say my name again." Turning her around, she saw tears in his eyes. While they hugged she called his name over and over again.

Hadn't he always been aware of the familiarity he had felt in this girl's presence, why hadn't he realised before? He held her tightly for a long moment hardly daring to believe she was real. How he had missed her after that summer.

Not knowing where she had come from or where she had gone. He had looked for her whenever he visited the many crofter's farmsteads. His lovely Kerry had invaded his dreams until he locked her in the deepest vaults of his mind.

A treasured boyhood memory. A special friend, oh, so special friend he had loved from the moment she had teased him in their first game of tag. Helen felt his arms tighten around her. Looking down at her now, this was his Kerry, that's how he had thought of her that summer. That torturous wonderful summer, she had healed his wounds with her friendship and her gay laughter and endless chatter and teasing. They had swum in the falls, and he had dried her hair. He had taught her to milk, and she had danced for him, and they had sat together under the stars along with the other children and been spellbound while they listened to the grownups. It was all there in the upturned face and laughing eyes.

Unable to help himself, he kissed her hard on the mouth. Her eyes registered the shock, briefly pulling away from him. The look of disbelief still in his eyes. Then leaning into him, the kiss more gentle becoming more passionate. Helen was in no doubt this was no boy of her memory; this was a man. Touching his face, she said, "I didn't know you straight away." He was hardly able to talk for the kisses, his eyes strange as they simmered with unleashed passion. She felt almost afraid.

James wrapped the tartan rug around Helen and slipped her shoes on her. She was shivering now. "It's my fault. I couldn't keep out of the water." James smiled lovingly. "Just like before, you were always in the water even when the weather was freezing." He had carried her to the Land Rover and found more blankets. "Which home do you want to go to?" sudden panic, she still hadn't told him about the Big House. "Mine or yours?"

"The lodge please, James." Then she buried herself in the blankets.

In the warm darkness, she saw again moonlight outlining the hills and the turf mounds. Her memory rang with the voices of happy children, bursts of songs, stories and laughter. The cattle and goats enjoying the fresh pastures, remembering how the men and women always had to be on the lookout for cattle raiders. Hugging the blankets closer, if only you could choose one day out of your life and make time stand still and relive that day again, just once. A sadness came over her knowing those times would never come again, wiping away a solitary tear making its way down her cheek. Pull yourself together, Helen, thinking it's time to get out of her wet clothes.

In the privacy of the plaid blanket, managing to take her wet top off and glad she had put her white sweater and maroon cord jacket in the Land Rover, she felt comfortable. Sliding into the front as the scenery rolled past, seeing the well-worn track she had noticed earlier on their way up. "Can we explore that way, where does it lead to." He hesitated, a slight furrow creasing his brow, then looking at her enquiring face, decided to turn left and drove for a short way.

Parking the Land Rover close to the hedge, they stood looking into the distance. The late evening sun was filtering through the trees, turning the lake gold. A gust of wind made a small whirlwind. "We will walk now." James helped her untangle herself from the blanket and stood looking at her; he was very quiet. Walking slowly on the well-worn pathway, Helen could now see stone mounds appearing every few yards. James had a strange look on his face and his mood seemed to have changed. A dark shadow slipped across her path and into the undergrowth taking her by surprise, James smiled as she came closer.

Noticing a large two-coloured stone, Helen picked it up wondering about its origin. Brushing the dust off it, she thought it had started off very large, but after a few earthquakes, it had been pushed out and laid there, probably millions of years old. It seemed to glitter in parts. They walked on.

James was watching her with interest. Pausing at a mound of stones, she tried to read the crumbling weatherworn piece of wood. "These stone mounds mark the route of old funeral processions." He could see by the surprised look she hadn't known. "See that large flat-topped boulder, that's where the relations would have rested the coffin before reaching the chosen burial place." Helen looked at the boulder then at James with a slightly puzzled expression. "You see, in the olden days, they believed the coffin must not touch the ground, or earth, in case the spirit escapes to wander restless forever before it reaches its cairn or monument." They had stopped, and he was staring as if without seeing at a stone mound. He had told her a little while ago that one of the sayings on a stone mound was: 'cur me clack air a charn' I will lay a stone of respect on his cairn whoever he is'.

Looking at the stone in her hand, she decided to place it on the mound they had stopped by. He was looking at the stone she had placed on this mound, then at her. She had the feeling she was intruding. "Shouldn't I have done that?" she said as she made to retrieve it, but the look on his face made her stop. In an instant, she knew that this mound profoundly disturbed him, that she had added her stone to. Bending closer to try to read the words on the plaque, weathered, it was unreadable; she heard James voice again. "I will lay a stone of respect on his cairn, whoever he is."

James took her hand and started to walk on. Opening her fingers, he put her hand to his lips and kissed the palm of her hand. In that moment, she knew it was his father's. How uncanny, she felt very strange. Helen could see and feel old sorrows weighed heavy on him. As they walked on, she listened to his voice feeling he was baring his soul. "Up here, I feel my father close." He was quiet for a moment. "Simple things I remember, when he would take my brother Stuart and me fishing and when we would watch him help a calf to be born. He would put milk straight from the cow's udder in a bowl, warm and creamy and let us drink." He turned his head towards her. "Sorry, I've been—"

"James, it's lovely remembering your family, go on." He had a different expression now.

"I loved my grandmother. I remember her spinning wool, the thin streams of spun wool flowing from her spindle." He smiled at her; he was back. In the distance could be seen a group of Jacob sheep and some highland cattle, and in the far distance the Atlantic Ocean, looking like a blue grey field.

Chapter 6

By 6.30 pm, Helen was curled up, feet under her looking a picture of health in her plaid dressing gown relating the day's happenings to Mary and Angus, in between stifling a yawn. "Oh, my dear girlie." Mary's face was shocked. "The falls are always ice cold any time of year, you'll catch your death Och, what made you stand so close; you're no twelve now, tch." She put Helen's clothes to soak. Angus had a bemused look.

"So you enjoyed reliving the past, lass?" He was looking straight ahead, as if remembering his own boyhood, that faraway look that she had seen in James's eyes.

Her smile confirmed he was right as he added, "Hope you don't mind, lass, but we accepted the invitation to the castle on your behalf."

"Oh, yes, Molly said day after tomorrow is very convenient for them." She dried her hands. A sleepy "fine, as Shakespeare said. Sleep per chance to dream".

Two days later saw them being driven by Helen in her wine Rover, to the castle. A large bunch of roses adorned the back seat. For some strange reason, Helen felt nervous. Having never met anyone from the castle although Mary spoke highly of them, she knew Aunt Matty had known them well. Twenty minutes had them entering the gates as the castle loomed in front of them. It looked much different up close than through the binoculars. One of the workmen pulled the iron gate open, making it shudder. Angus spoke as they passed. Then another high six-bar gate that looked quite new was rolled open quietly by a gardener working nearby. Helen was surprised to see ornamental urns full of flowering shrubs. "Pull right up to the door, Helen." She did as she was bade and saw a rosy face woman at the large entrance. "Molly, we broughtHelen to see you." The two women greeted each other fondly, and to Helen's surprise, she was greeted the same. Angus slid his hat off and wedging it under his arm kissed Molly on the cheek, retrieving the roses from the car.

The lounge they were now sitting in was cool with long drapes at the wide windows and giant oil paintings that stretched almost to the floor. Mary ushered Helen towards the very attractive woman who had just stood up. "This is the late Matilda's niece, Helen." A dainty hand was extended. Helen smiled as the wide intelligent eyes observed her with a faint smile.

"Katriana, and I'm pleased to meet you at last." Looking directly into her face, Helen knew this lady was not of Scottish blood, with high cheekbones, slender neck and eyelashes to die for. "This is my first visit to the castle." The sound of hooves and voices echoed in the courtyard. "That will be my sons returning from checking the boundaries." Helen held her breath as in through the door came a young man with dark hair and striking good looks and kissed his mother.

Looking around he said, "Good to see you, Angus, Mary," making Mary laugh as he kissed her on the neck and whispered in her ear.

"Och, ye canny lad," she said tapping his arm. He stood up straight looking at Helen appreciatively. "What have we here? Is she family?" Angus nodded. "This is Helen – Stuart."

Stuart walked slowly towards her. "I knew she was family as soon as I saw those good looks." He put both arms around her and bent her into (what her dance friends would have called) a film star kiss. As he stood her up and she recovered, she saw James standing at the door. Glaring at his brother, he came over to Helen; she had one each side of her. Taking a quick look at Angus in the hope of some support, she only saw him raise his eyebrows slightly but was amused.

"I think you have already met James." His mother got up. "Come with me, we're going to enjoy a drink with my nephew's wife." She suddenly linked arms with Mary. "Getting excited, we have a new baby due in a couple of months." The two women walked on talking companionably. The boys had disappeared, and Helen linked arms with Angus and followed the ladies only stopping to look at some large oil paintings.

The rest of the afternoon passed pleasantly; Molly joined the group when she brought tea, sandwiches and cake, and Helen took to Ginty and was sure they would become good friends. The conversation turned to horses and prize bulls, and Angus offered to take Helen for a peep at them.

As they made their way to the bullpens, Angus said, "Well, now you know who he is, lassie. He's the laird of the castle with lots of responsibilities, and I'm dinna glad you're gonna get on well with Ginty; she's a lovely lass but not much female company. Don't worry your head about Stuart; he's always been the same, a forward little colt acting like a young stallion." In the dimness of the pens, Helen was taken aback by the size of the bulls; their names were over the top of their doors. First was 'Lakeland Lover' looking comfortable as he scratched his head on a post. Then 'Out of The Blue', enormous, with horns almost as wide as the pen. "This is 'Lady of the Loch'." Angus rubbed her forehead. That's Out of the Blue's mother; she's in calf and if it's as good as the big boy…" His voice trailed off as they could hear raised voices further along the building.

"I don't want to fall out with you, Stuart, but – back off." Stuart's face broke into a slow grin.

"You're serious about this girl, well, well, James." Cavalier blew down his nose and shook his head, breaking the tension for a moment between them. "You know me, James, girls are for loving." This was followed by a good-natured laugh.

"Yes, I do know you," James said through clenched teeth, "and there's a few broken hearts in the glen already. Just don't even try it."

"Don't try to tell me what I can do or can't do." Stuart's voice now had an edge of anger to it. James's eyes flashed a fiery warning in his brother's direction.

Angus and Helen watched a whirlwind of dust slant across the stony yard. The outward scene of rugged beauty and contentment gave no indication to the fury that raged between the two men. Helen and Angus made their way quietly back to the comfort of Ginty and Andrew's home in the wing of the castle, certain they hadn't been seen. While saying their goodbyes Helen agreed to take Ginty to the nearest town for a 'girls' few hours' out and some slightly looser clothes, seeing the envious looks of the other three women, it became a five girls' outing, the following week.

The 'Girls' day out turned into a shopping trip to choose things for the coming 'Ball'. Lunch had been booked into the imposing Glen Fife Hotel with its man on the door and its smartly turned out waiters and waitresses. White tablecloths and tartan centrepiece gave the whole place the feeling of luxury, and the happy party of chattering women soon settled to studying the menu. Ginty was beginning to feel tired so Helen said her and Ginty would have coffee in the park near where she had parked the Rover and wait for the others.

"Are you pleased with your dress?" Ginty gave her a wide tired smile.

"I love it, and it's Andrew's favourite colour," she said peeping in the carrier and pulling a corner of the pale peach lace. "I've enjoyed today, thank you, Helen, and, surprise surprise, Katriana doesn't mix much, not since her husband's death over ten years ago now. It was so good to see her – mixing in and laughing with us. Usually, she's a bit shy and excuses herself away from company."

Helen found her a small stall to put her feet up on, as she'd noticed her ankles were looking a little puffy. "You know, my Aunt Matty would have loved today." Without realising it, Helen found herself opening up to her, as the time flew past. They were on their second cup of coffee as the other three joined them at the table and all started talking at once.

Katriana took Helen's aside, as she delivered her, Molly and Ginty to the castle. "I really have enjoyed today, being with all the ladies." Helen suddenly felt sorry for her; she seemed so vulnerable. She searched in her bag, handing Helen a small parcel. "This is for you." The surprised look on Helen's face almost rendered her speechless. Arriving at the lodge, Helen left Mary to tell Angus all about their day out and she ran upstairs to hang, with great excitement, her dress up. The ball was in three days' time, and she hadn't seen or heard from James. Then, taking her small parcel, she went to sit in the kitchen of Angus and Mary.

They sat, with interested expectancy as Helen undid the small parcel, carefully folding back the tissue to reveal a sparkling spray of jewelled flowers to be worn as a hair adornment. Helen held it to her hair. Angus's eyes sparkled like the stones in the curved flowers. "You'll look a picture, and there'll be no shortages of partners for you, girlie, and that's a fact." Helen handed it over for closer inspection. Mary held it up to her hair and it looked lovely even in Mary's grey hair. "Are you no going to show me yer frocks, you two?"

"No, we're not, Angus McGreger; you'll just have to wait until the ball."

"Well, are they long?"

"Uh."

"Are they short?"

"Uh."

"Backless?"

"Uh."

"Frontless, oh, away with ye woman. The Strawbetties are calling for water." He left closing the door quietly behind him. Mary and Helen laughed over the washing up.

"The canny man, where does he get such notions, backless, frontless, at least he didna say topless." They started laughing again. "The sasanack." Helen was tempted to ask Mary how much wine she had today.

It was a windy morning; the garage had rung to say they would be delivering the Land Rover in a couple of hours, and Helen decided when it arrived she would take it for a quick drive. One of the farmsteads she had been meaning to visit on her aunt's list, and it was the nearest, saw her motoring towards the far hills. An hour later, she pulled up at a poor-looking low building. Two children playing outside the door, ran in as they saw her and came out pulling their mother to the door; she ushered them in and pulled the door to and stood and waited. Helen gave a cheery hello and introduced herself. The woman looked tired and drawn. "I canny pay, not yet." Helen went to say something, but there was a voice from inside. The woman turned and went in. Helen stood wondering what to do, a grubby little face peeped around the door and opened it a little wider. Helen went in.

The woman was cradling a very thin body and giving sips of water. A small child standing looking at her as she chewed her sleeve said quietly, "Daddy's dying." The woman turned her head and put her finger to her lips 'shh'. In shock, Helen left the room and found herself in a small shabby kitchen but scrubbed clean. Through a small window, she could see her brand new Land Rover and felt a sob leave her.

A few minutes later, she sat talking to the woman, her face was expressionless, as she heard her say, "Ay, ye can put boots on the bairn's feet, but ye canna put flesh back on bones, and I can no pay." Lifting her apron, she hid her face in it and sobbed.

Driving back to the lodge, Helen's mind was in turmoil, how could this happen; she supposed this woman had been too proud to ask for help. Diverting to the solicitors and then the bank, she thought she would have to do a lot more thinking. This was her land and her people, so the responsibility was down to her, but it didn't make her feel much better as she walked into the doctor's. Still, she had done all she could for the moment.

Sitting in the garden with Angus, she talked it over with him. He knew of the family she spoke but not their plight. "Och, lass, we're a proud race, and it can be our undoin, but ye puttin things to right, let me know what way I kin help." Looking at her sad face he said, "Think o sumat a wee more cheerful, it's the ball tomorrow, why Mary is talking of nothin else, lass."

Opening her wardrobe, she looked at the cream and gold ball gown, but somehow she could only see the frayed sleeves of the children and the apron covering the sobbing woman's face. Hearing a car, she opened her window and seeing tanned arms and dark hair, she ran lightly down the stairs. Disguising her disappointment, she greeted Stuart. "Helen, I've come to invite you to be my partner at the ball – you will go to the ball, Cinderella. I'll pick you up about—"

"Whoa, whoa, just a minute, Stuart, I'm not going with any partners. I'll see you all at the ball."

"Well, who's taking you then?"

There was a short pause and a manly deep voice said, "I am." Angus put a box of strawberries into Stuart's hands. "Give these to the ladies, son." On her way in, she kissed Angus on the cheek. "Has James no asked ye, lass?"

She shook her head. "Not really."

"I'm sure he meant to." Mary spoke in a quiet tone. "I'll no say anything on the matter but how can a man let something like this slip his mind. Ah, well, it's his loss. Wait till he sees your wee dress, he'll come running, but he'll have to go to the back of the queue, but I'll say no more…If—"

Angus broke in. "Mary," then smiling, "I thought you weren't going to have anything to say on the matter."

"Well, I didn't, and Angus McGregor, make sure you are the first one to dance with our Helen." Angus went to say something. "Oh, and make sure after Helen…I'm first." He was looking at her with affection. "And then…and then Molly, no – perhaps Katriana, then Molly." Helen put her arms around Mary.

"Well, that's that sorted."

Chapter 7

As Mary, Angus and Helen entered the ballroom, the sheer sight of it made them all gasp. The wonderful array of ball gowns and some of the men in kilts, there were men in evening suits and soft lilting music. Helen saw Ginty waving and they made their way towards her; she looked so elegant in her dress of peach lace and peach skin to match. They greeted each other and Angus sat Mary next to Molly. Both women looked lovely in soft flowing silks and wrist flowers. Helen was looking around as Stuart skated up to her. "Looking for me?" Smiling, he slipped an arm around her waist.

"No, your mother actually, and will you not hang on to me," she said pulling his arm away.

"Mother has to sit with the chief Piper." He waved in no particular direction. Helen could tell he had already consumed plenty. Feeling a hand on her elbow, she knew instinctively it was James and reached up to kiss him on the cheek. He looked so handsome; she felt the same weakness as he steered her to a chair, appraising the cream and gold flowing dress with his eyes.

"I think the jewel in your hair is lovely." Then Helen saw a frown cross his brow.

He looked at her strangely for a long time, then bent and spoke softly in her ear. "What have you done to your hair?" Now where had she heard that before? Touching the neat shorter tresses, she knew she didn't look like something out of Swan Lake, that was for sure. His eyes were steady on her and his expression thoughtful. He was remembering the way she had looked the first time he had seen her. Hair swept up, hanging childlike as she paddled in the burn. She could feel his eyes on her; his expression was unreadable. He was thinking how her hair had tumbled over his arm as he knelt beside her on the heather.

Sighing, he instinctively touched his breast pocket at the memory, even though he had asked Ginty to put the rose in her flower press for him. "You look different, that's all." Feeling snubbed, she turned her back on him, giving her head a small shake so that he had the benefit of its shapely style.

"Well, I like it and that's all that matters really." One eyebrow raised momentarily, but he made no comment. Helen gave him a wide smile then concentrated on the company. Stuart appeared from nowhere and tugged at her arm.

"You promised to dance with me." And before she knew it, she was being led around the dance floor by a very determined Stuart. When the music stopped, a group of people sang 'Haste ye Back', the song must have been heard clear across the glen. Stuart walked her off the floor with his arm tightly around her. Helen was relieved to sit down; the music started up again, and Helen reached for her drink, but her hand was taken by James, and without a word, she was whisked once again onto the dance floor.

His eyes blazed down at her, his grip firm, swinging her a little too energetically around the ballroom until she could hardly breathe. When the music slowed and dancers began to leave the floor with a swishing of skirts, laughing and chatting in the enjoyable atmosphere, she smiled up at him, but before she could ask to please not hold her quite so tightly next time, he swept her off the floor. "I suppose you are enjoying yourself." His face showing no emotion, she felt the prickle in her throat, this was unlike him, and she wondered what had brought about this dark mood.

Deciding not to be part of his mood, she replied brightly, "Yes, I am, very much." And to prove it, she beamed, looking around her at the colourful throng.

The music started up again, a lilting waltz, and James held her to him a little more gentler this time. Helen was relishing having a dance floor this big to swirl around; she looked up at the chandelier; it was making the centre of the ornate ceiling sparkle.

As they danced past their group, Stuart called out with a provocative catch in his voice and raised his glass. "Your good health, Helen, the next dance is mine." Her feet hardly had time to touch the floor before they were on the other side of the ballroom. Having to really stretch her legs against his taut body and long strides, she was now finding it a little difficult to keep up with him.

"You are a very good dancer." He held her a little way from him for a moment and looked at her. The compliment was unexpected. She looked at him amused.

"Well, thank you." She was pleased that the pace had slowed, but there was no chance for conversation, as his arm around her and his hand firmly in the small of her back was pulling her to him. Helen breathed the warm manly aroma and was acutely aware of the contours of his body as the pressure of his upper legs moved them expertly between other dancers.

From somewhere above her head, she heard him say, "You must feel quite at home." She suddenly went cold, knowing she hadn't conversed with him yet about the 'Big House'. Of course, she had meant to, then the niggle returned. Determined to enjoy every minute of this glittering occasion, as the music slowed to finish, she lifted his arm above her head, deftly spun under it and dropped to a deep curtsey, causing the beautiful dress to lay in folds around her. James had been taken by surprise but smiled and did a slight bow. Helen looked radiant, and as she rose, James felt his heart miss a beat. He'd lost this wonderful creature once a long time ago, but he wasn't going to let it happen again. He would try to shake off these dark thoughts. Vowing to have a brotherly chat with Stuart.

During the evening, Helen had no shortage of partners, dancing with Angus for the Scottish reel, amazed at the ease he moved, followed by a dance that required the ladies on the inside circle to pass on to the next man in a progression. Laughing and eyes sparkling being turned and moved on the succession of partners was many, James, Andrew, Stuart, the ferryman and many more being finally led from the floor by a breathless fresh-faced young man who thanked her profusely.

She sank into the chair next to Ginty as Andrew came up behind his wife and kissed her saying, "You'll be able to do this soon," clasping her hands.

Ginty smiled at him and shifted her position, turning to Helen. "You've got to be fit to stay the pace." As Helen was getting her breath back, she handed her drink and both girls laughed.

"I'm so enjoying this, Ginty, I've missed dancing."

"You're quite pink." Helen's hands felt her face.

"I didn't know it would be as good as this."

Looking around, Helen was relieved to see Stuart nowhere to be seen, breathed a sigh of relief and relaxed into the chair. Nearby a group of men chatted, among them was James, regarding her from time to time. Helen turned her attention to Ginty as Mary came over. "Och, you wee girlies look so lovely tonight. Have ye told her about the surprise in store for her?"

Helen's eyes widened. "Och, well, I'll no spoil it." Helen thought how tasteful Mary looked as she walked away, was suddenly sad thinking how her mother and father would have enjoyed this affair but was brought out of her sadness by the surprise of a piper appearing at the top of the broad stairway. The sound wafted down through the ballroom and a hush descended on the dancers as the lights dimmed. It was haunting and sad, then growing in volume until the skirl of the pipes made her blood curdle as she thought of the enormous pictures depicting the ferocious battles. Watching the audience, their faces told the feeling this was evoking in them. In the dim light, the piper played on. After a while, the piper started to descend the stairs as the lights gradually went up and gasps and clapping as the men in full regalia, their kilts in all the different family tartans swishing. Helen put her hand to her mouth and felt tears burning. The sight of all the colour and music was almost overwhelming; she caught her breath; there on the stairs was Andrew, Stuart and James. She felt Ginty's hand on her arm as she handed her a hanky.

"I didn't see them leave…When…" Ginty laughed. "Helen, now sit back and enjoy."

Girls in white flowing dresses with a tartan sash over one shoulder were entering the floor now and partnering the men. The dancers acknowledged each other and stood motionless. Helen sat spellbound. The dance began.

An hour later after a succession of dances, Helen remembered when Lucinder Balentine had shown her around and told her to look at the pictures in the first three rooms of the first floor when the ball was on. Ginty had wanted her to wait for James, but Helen finished her drink and said she wouldn't be long. She mounted the broad staircase and stopped half way up to look back on the swirling colours below. It was certainly a grand affair. Along the upper hall taking in the huge pictures, she was suddenly glad of the rest from dancing, and the added pressure of Stuart's over-attentiveness. Helen knew it was just to annoy his brother, but he hadn't bothered her for a while now.

An unusual carved candle stand graced a curve in the wall, further along the light shone on a suite of armour. Helen stood looking at it, touching the thick chain metal near the waist of the suit, and it occurred to her that the man that wore it must be a giant; she shivered. High on the wall hung claymores and broad swords of battle, knowing the weapons would have been used unmercifully by men with revenge in their hearts, remembering the stories of how the mists of the glen still weep for the wasted warrior giants.

Opening the heavy door to a stately sitting room, there was a rosy glow from one corner table lamp. It served only to outline the largeness of the room. Closing the door, she leaned against it for a moment feeling enveloped in silence. Picking her way carefully across the room, she stood in front of the marble mantle. The light picked up the gilt edges of a mirror, which reached to the ceiling; it reflected her outline. Letting her head drop back, she breathed deeply and decided that whatever happened she would not let anything spoil this wonderful evening. She told her reflection, "I am just going to rise above it." A deep chuckle from a low sofa made her almost jump out of her skin.

"I hadn't realised you were into levitation." She knew the voice from the darkness was Stuart as he swung his legs from the sofa and stood up. "Is my brother giving you a hard time?"

"I'm sorry, Stuart, I didn't know you were in here." She just caught sight of a young girl making for the door. Helen called after her 'don't go' fervently wishing she knew where the lights were, not wanting to be left alone with Stuart. He was unsteady on his feet and grinning sleepily at her. "Look, I didn't mean to…" But she got no further. As the door opened flooding the immediate surroundings with light, she saw the girl slip out and James fill the doorway. He saw the relief on her face. Stuart, realising his brother was watching, put his arms about Helen's waist and pulled her to him. He was as strong as an ox even though he was full of too much highland cheer. He was slurring.

"Darling, there are plenty more fish in the lochs, as we say hear in Scotland." He held on to Helen to stop himself from falling over. "I'm going to see a pretty pretty girl like you gets home safely." He was leaning on her heavily.

Gradually walking to the door, Helen said, "Thank you, Stuart, that's very kind of you." She extracted herself from his grasp. "But I am home."

Now in the light of the doorway she told him, "I'm going to see that you get home safely." His surprise was evident.

"Now you're talking sense, my lovely." He patted her arm. "Told you, James – they're putty in my hands." James made no attempt to move as Helen and Stuart swaying slightly drew level with him. He stood, displeasure plainly showing on his face. Helen carefully took Stuart's arm and linked it into James's arm.

"There, safe and sound your big brother won't let any harm come to you." She squeezed past James. "And I have no intention of leaving this wonderful occasion just yet. I'm having too much fun." Blowing them a kiss, she swept along to the staircase, looking back smiled to herself at the astonished looks on their faces, and they hadn't moved. She waved as she descended the stairs. "Good night, gentlemen." Stopping she added, "Oh and James, about Sunday, I accept." Walking daintily down the last few stairs, she was unaware of the laughter in James's eyes or the returned kiss that followed her. Helen couldn't resist a few dance spins on this wonderful floor drawing a few claps from other dancers.

Making her way to where Katriana was sitting, Helen thanked her for the gift. James's mother smiled. "I'm glad you like it. I noticed the dance spins, Helen, very professional, so at some time you must have been a dancer and studied ballet." Helen began to talk about her love for dancing and how she hadn't grown tall enough. Katriana clasped her hands together and looked almost excited. "Helen, I was a Russian ballerina." Helen sat down while she told her story. It appears while over here performing in Edinburgh she fell in love with the most handsome man in the country. The laird himself.

Looking at her glowing face as she spoke of her love of dance and her wonderful husband, Helen thought about the portrait of the man with the twinkling eyes, their happiness cut short. For a moment, it cast a shadow over the evening, but they had known a great love and happiness, of that Helen was sure.

Letting her eyes travel around the colourful sparkling ballroom coming to rest on James, she knew also that she had fallen in love with the most handsome man, the laird himself.

Chapter 8

David Balentine had called in to the lodge with a bottle of wine and to tell Angus he was on his way to the castle to meet James, Stuart and Andrew as they were all off to a meeting of cattle breeders. "I have to dash as it's getting a bit near take off time for the helicopter. Lucinder said she will pop in later, Mary, if that's all right."

"That's good, David, did you enjoy yourself last night?" He chuckled his infectious laugh.

"Mary my love, I wish we still had it to come." He sighed. "The clearing up team had just arrived as I came out; they were patting balloons about and having a rare old time…All good fun. I'll come in and tell you how we get on this evening." Angus walked to the door with him.

"I wish you luck, David, it would be nice to come up with a solution on the rustling." He waved as he pulled away in his shining Mustang.

Helen woke slowly, knowing she had slept late. Still recovering from the night of the ball, she stretched luxuriously reliving the enjoyable night and hoping it would be repeated next year or perhaps sooner.

Mary had been busy knitting for the new baby, soon to be born to Ginty and Andrew, James's cousin and wife and little two-year-old Duncan. The faint aroma of breakfast made Helen sit up in bed, looking at the clock. Rousing herself reluctantly, she went over to the window to enjoy the vista and breathe the morning freshness of the highlands. In the distance, she caught a glimpse of a helicopter rising from the castle grounds, remembering it was the men's meeting today.

It didn't seem cold, but it was overcast, and still in a dream state, she lifted down the parcel of baby clothes she had bought on their girls' day out. Soft all in ones, two nightwears with button up bottoms and an adorable nursery hanging to keep the baby amused. Looking at the dainty garments was making her broody. Feeling her tummy rumbling, she started to take off her nightclothes, dreamily folding them.

Taking her time, Helen showered and dressed casually then set about wrapping the presents, keeping an attractive wrapping for Mary's delicately patterned shawl and little pure white cardigans. Helping herself to scrambled eggs and toast, she settled herself at the table.

Mary looked at her amused, as Helen was eating with her eyes closed. "Are ye no going to the castle today, lass?" There was a pause…

"I'm sorry, Mary, you're talking in my sleep." This was followed by a stifled yawn.

"James was here earlier." Suddenly, Helen was wide awake. "I told him you were still asleep, he didna want to disturb ye." Helen leaned back rubbing her eyes.

"Was there a message."

"No." Helen blinked. "No as in nothing?"

"He was in the Land Rover; he'd just popped in for a wee while." Putting her knitting down, she poured Helen's drink. "He said how much the family and him in particular enjoyed the ball." Mary paused with the teapot gazing at the ceiling. "Ay, it was a grand affair, no doubt about it." Coming back to the present, she carried on pouring Helen's drink.

Helen put the presents in the Land Rover as Angus handed her a box of strawberries for the castle. As it turned out, it wasn't a good day for Ginty. As soon as Helen saw her, she thought she looked tired and was in obvious discomfort with her back. Saying she wouldn't stop for long after handing over the presents, thinking they had enough to do and Ginty needed to be in bed but wouldn't hear of it.

"Come and talk to me, Helen." Molly was relieved and went off to do a few jobs until the tea tray arrived. Katriana had delivered little Duncan to his other grandparents for a few days and then carried on to fife for a short stay with a dancer friend. Helen thought perhaps a bit of company was what the pregnant girl needed, so smiling cheerfully, she sat herself in an armchair opposite her.

"How are you today, Ginty?"

The girl just waved a tired hand. Looking at her, Helen felt a surge of compassion for her; she looked so young. Andrew had married his college sweetheart when she was nineteen, and little Duncan had been born the following year.

The glass doors of the lounge at the lodge stood wide open, the heavy curtains moving a little. Gentle laughter pervaded across the garden, and the swaying roses looked as though they were enjoying it too.

Mary and Lucinder Balentine were enjoying the comfort of the armchairs and looked relaxed. Angus was pouring the wine that Lucinder had brought, bringing roses to their cheeks and bursts of laughter recalling how the evening had progressed. It was an outstanding success. Two lots of musicians had stayed overnight and the ladies were laughing at the fact that they played this morning for the cleaning team, very entertaining.

"Oh, Mary, if only I were a bit younger, I would have joined in all the dancing. I must say all you ladies looked lovely." For no reason at all, there was another peal of laughter. Angus was smiling broadly, as he handed a plate of biscuit and cake to them. Mary wiped her eyes.

"Didn't the highland dancers do us proud, and at least Stuart stayed on his feet; he can be quite…naughty." Another burst of laughter.

"I thought the cartwheel he attempted was quite good." More laughter.

"What time are you expecting David back from the cattle men's meeting?"

"Early evening he said." The mood turned quiet. "David had a visit from a breeder. Another theft, it was his champion Aberdeen, Angus, and he was very upset, as he had spent a lot of money on making his place burglar-proof." Angus was shaking his head. "Come on, ladies, let's go and smell the roses." They went through the open doors as a balloon floated down the drive. The group stopped, then another light-hearted laughter floated after it. "What be your favourite colour of roses, Lucinder?" Angus took his secateurs from his pocket. Both women together said 'pink' and turning to go into the lodge. They were laughing again. Angus thought the ball had been good for everyone; he certainly had a feel good feeling, as he cut some of his favourite roses for Lucinder.

Watching the two of them go in through the glass doors, he heard his Mary say, "I'll be putting the kettle on, make sure you wash your hands." More laughter.

Helen was relieved the boisterous little two-year-old was away at his grandmother's, at least his mother was able to rest.

Ginty shifted in her chair, pushing a cushion into the middle of her back, rubbing her aching body before settling. Looking at the girl's swollen figure and flushed face, Helen asked, "Would a nice cold drink be helpful?" A grateful nod sent her hurrying to the kitchen with Ginty's voice saying 'don't be long', in the background. Molly pulled her chair nearer the girl, patting her arm.

Hurrying along the corridor, Helen wasn't at all sure she knew where the kitchen was, this was only her third visit to the castle, and she was shown the upper rooms. Passing one of the studies, Helen got together a tray with a selection of fruit drinks and an ice bucket on it and hurried back to the young girl. Molly looked in surprise. "You were quick." Helen carefully put the tray down and smiled at Ginty.

"Well, I had two choices, either get lost (shrugging her shoulders at Molly) or raid the first suitable room." She smiled at the girl. "At your service, ma'am."

The three of them sat sipping the cool drink, as Ginty arched her back and slipped another pillow behind her. "I suppose I've been lucky really, just sailed through my pregnancy, it's just these last couple of days with this nagging backache I just can't get comfortable," she said putting her hand in the small of her back. "I don't remember being this bad with Duncan."

"Oh, well," Helen said brightly, "perhaps this one is a girl." She sat back. "One of the girls I danced with in Chorus Line was actually born in a theatre dressing room." She smiled at the girl. "How long will it be now?"

"Exactly twenty-three days and they can't go quick enough for me."

Helen went to the window and looked at the sky. "I wonder how the cattle men's meeting went. When I was at the Balentines in the Big House, she mentioned how worried her husband had been about some cattle rustling." Molly tut-tutted.

"We always have to be alert these days, something new, that's why the boys have brought the prize bulls nearer home. Didna happen in my day." Ginty pushed her hair back from her face.

"Tell me some more about your dancing days, if this one is a girl, you can teach her to dance for me."

Helen came away from the window and pushed a stool under Ginty's feet, settling herself and delving into her unending store of theatre stories, drawing laughter from her eager listeners, the time passed pleasantly.

Molly was just putting the tea tray down when Ginty suddenly pushed the stool away with her foot and sat up stiffly. Molly and Helen looked at her as the colour seemed to drain from her face, and she drew a breath in through closed teeth. "There, there, lass, that back is being troublesome."

"I think I'll go and lie down; it's not giving me any rest; in fact, it's worse."

Standing up gingerly, she took a few steps then her knees buckled under her, and she let out a strangled moan. The two women darted forward and supported the heavily pregnant Ginty under her arms, but the girl didn't want to straighten. Resting the trembling figure against her, Helen tried to soothe away the frightened look in her eyes.

Whispering sobs were coming from Ginty now. "No. Please no…it's too." Soon Molly stood up.

"Dear God." She shot Helen a look. "Stay there." And she flew from the room. Obeying the older woman, she stayed put, but Ginty looked so uncomfortable, crouched on one knee, her head buried into Helen's shoulder. Surely, she would be more comfortable laying down. Coaxing the girl to lay on the floor, between spasms of pain, she managed to get her comfortable with a pillow under her head and two or three under her legs. And as another pain came, Helen discreetly looked at her watch. Molly hurried back in. "It's all right, child, doctor's on his way, fifteen minutes at the most," she said and got down on her knees. Helen saw that Molly was panting, but she smiled at her and said, "You'll have to be a helping me up from here in a wee while." She spread a soft rug over the anxious Ginty. The girl's face was ashen in spite of the pain; she was quiet for the moment. Molly patted her hand reassuringly.

"I'm in labour. Molly, it's definitely labour. What am I going to do?" Her voice trailed away in a sob as she was caught by another more fierce pain. Fear passed through Helen; she felt so inadequate.

Moving along the carpet, she slipped Ginty's shoes off then went back to her head. "You'll be all right." Molly attempted a laugh. "Of course, she'll be all right, haven't I had five bairns of my own." She looked across at the window in the vain hope of seeing a car coming over the rise. In the forefront of her mind was the fact that this bairn was three weeks early.

The two women's eyes met, and Molly mouthed silently, "Oh, I'm so glad you're here." Then she stroked the soft wisps of hair back from Ginty's face as she gritted her teeth in readiness for another pain. Helen indicated quietly that it was only a minute and a half since the last pain. Helen helped Molly up; she left the room saying she wouldn't be a moment.

"Molly…Molly," she said as she felt another pain coming. "Don't leave me." Helen held onto the girl's hands and massaged the middle of her back between pains. Molly appeared behind a stash of white towels.

"Doctor will need these, and I've put two of the large kettles on low."

"Now, Helen, when you see the doctor's emergency headlights come over the rise, I want you to run as fast as you can and open all the doors – all of them mind and leave them open and the gates and be sure to shut the big gate as soon as the doc's through." Ginty couldn't have picked a worse time to go into labour. Katriana was away for the next few days, and all three men had taken off early this morning in the helicopter. The cattle breeder's meetings were unpredictable in hours, but Helen had the feeling they should have been back by now. Ginty cried out and rolled onto her side. Agitation was making Helen's stomach ache; she tried not to show it. Rubbing the pregnant girl's back, she felt her relax for a moment.

"Everything is going to be all right, Ginty, your being so brave, doctor will be here soon now." Fervently hoping he would, she wished now with all her heart the men were here too. Not that they could have been much help, but Ginty could have been lifted into bed; she jumped as she heard Molly shout.

"Off you go then, there's the emergency headlights."

Helen took off like the wind, taking the stairs two at a time, opening the doors wide as she tore through the hallways. Then the big door, once in the spacious courtyard running as fast as she could to the huge eight-bar gate, wedging it back firmly. Then ran on to the iron ornamental gate pulling the creaking complaining structure as wide as it would go. Helen wondered for a moment why it had already been left half open, sighing, she lent on the gate to get her breath back, knowing the car was not far away.

The doctor's car hurtled into the courtyard and up to the open doorway. Helen breathed a sigh of relief; she'd never been more pleased to see anyone in her life, at this moment, than that wonderful, wonderful man. Everything would be all right now. Nothing could have been further from the truth.

Putting her hands on the scrolled iron work, she started to push the heavy gate fully closed. The twelve-foot high gate was hard work, and she paused halfway trying to get a better grip on the shuddering iron; it was then that she noticed a small horsebox tight up against the hedge along the drive. Pausing, she realised she could hear something; it was just a drone in the far distance and Helen's heart leapt; she knew they wouldn't be able to see her yet, but in her excitement, she started waving and calling and pointing to the castle. "Oh, Andrew, hurry, hurry up or you'll miss it." Helen knew there was a flag in the barn, and she was going to wave it.

The split second before she blacked out, Helen was acutely aware of stale whisky and vile body odour. Spinning into the black well of unconsciousness, she knew she had been hit hard on the side of the head; she was aware of voices around her but then, oblivion. "Move yer great arss; we gotta get outa ear, we ain't got all day." A growl from one of the men.

"Your idea to do it in daylight."

"Shut yer face and move er, I told yer the big nobbs would be out the way terday, ear, ow ard did you it er."

"You saw er, wavin the alarm signal didn't ya and shoutin."

"Well, she ain't shoutin now."

"Look, we got one, let's get outer ear." They hurried to the horsebox. "You be goin ta take it steady or you'll break its four legs before yer get anywhere." The horsebox roared away in a cloud of dust. Minutes later, the helicopter landed inside the walls of the castle. David jumped out first bidding them goodbye and making for his car. Andrew had seen the doctor's car parked outside the wide open door and was running to the entrance. James was looking around puzzled; they had seen the horsebox travelling along the castle roadway on their way in.

James called across to his brother, "Stuart, were you expecting anyone?" They walked together to close the gate; Stuart shook his head.

"I'm as puzzled as you. I know Andrew has been looking at ponies for Duncan, but he would have said if he had found one." The men walked across the courtyard suddenly noticing the outer door to the prize bulls was open. They both started to run and stopped at the door seeing the centre bullpen open and empty. "Out of the Blue's gone, James," Stuart almost screamed. "James, did you hear me? Out of the Blue's gone."

"I hear you." James walked into the empty pen, not believing. Stuart was cursing loudly and snatched up the flag instantly dropping to his knees crouching over and speaking softly to the crumpled figure. "Helen, Helen, what have they done to you." In one movement, Stuart had lifted her and rested her head on his shoulder watching a slow river of blood trickle across the creases of her eye and across her cheek. James was consumed with a double fury as he looked at her and had a sudden feeling of his father, what would he have done in this situation.

He walked behind Stuart looking into Helen's face and could feel himself shaking inside. Helen was whispering into Stuart's neck, "James, the baby…the doctor…I…"

"Shh now, everything is all right." He adjusted his grip on her.

"I knew you would find me, James." She slipped an arm around Stuart's neck and covered his cheek with weak kisses. The sight of the half-unconscious Helen so comfortable in the arms of his brother, even though he couldn't hear what she was saying, brought back the memories of them dancing at the ball. Stuart's voice broke across his anger.

"It's a bit of luck Ginty needed the doc, let's get her in quick."

"You call it luck?" Stuart looked at his brother's scowling face and put his manner down to shock.

Ginty had been moved to her and Andrew's bedroom now and Stuart went to lay Helen on one of the sofas, but James intervened and took her from Stuart making for his own room with a tearful Molly behind him. "What's happened, Helen went to open all the doors and gates for the doctor, and she never came back, oh, look at the side of her head."

An hour later, Helen was sitting up in bed, a large gauze dressing on the side of her head, a very sore elbow and a bruised shoulder already turning pretty colours, as Molly put it, sipping a cup of warm sweet tea. "Well, that's all I remember, Molly. I must admit I have a thumping headache – a bit woozy."

"That's the medicine the doctor gave you; he'll be up again in a minute."

"Molly, I need a bath, would you run one for me?"

"What in the world are ye be a thinkin of, lassie, no, I will not."

"Molly, you saw my clothes."

"Yes and I've got them a soakin now; you stay right where you are. If the doctor says so, then I'll do it, but I'll sit in there with you, lordy be, what would Mary and Angus be a thinkin of me." Helen had to smile; she thought a lot of Molly and the poor woman was looking tired and still looking after others,

"Molly, you've had quite a day."

"Yes, and it's no over yet." But her smile told Helen she was enjoying the – here and now.

The doctor gave permission for her to have a bath on the understanding that Molly sat in the bathroom with her. While the bath was filling Helen could hear her going through the assortment of bottles on the shelf and soon the tangy aroma she associated with James filled the moist air. Molly sat with a stack of white towels and a magazine, nearby was a very large robe.

Submerged in the large bath, knowing it was James, gave her a special feeling. The aromas now filling the room were intoxicating. Laying back, the water reaching her chin was very enjoyable. Her elbow throbbed. The bedroom door opened, and Andrew called Molly to come and see his new son; she bustled over and went into raptures. "Tell Helen I'll come back later." Molly was all smiles. "Oh, the bairn's gorgeous." She sighed and waited patiently for Helen to let out the bath water.

She helped her on with the very large navy robe. "Do you feel better fer that, I think you should be off your feet, lass. Mary and Angus have arrived to see you and the wee new baby."

"Thanks for all your help, Molly."

"Aw, away into bed with you now."

Angus sat on the side of the bed while Mary busied about laying clothes over a chair near the bed. "I've brought one of your cheery frocks, lass." Mary's voice was bright, and Helen was pleased to see her.

She smiled when she saw the rainbow-coloured dress and aran cardigan through the plastic. Wasn't that just like her, Helen thought. Mary placed a pretty velvet bag on the seat of the chair, patting it she said, "Here's some bits and bobs."

Chapter 9

James opened his bedroom door for the doctor to do a final check on Helen. Closing it, he leaned against the figured wood. "How's my patient?" The doctor reached across the bed and looked closely at Helen's eyes with his pencil light. "Still feeling the headache, lass?" She smiled and nodded.

"But it's not so bad since I've taken the tablets, thanks."
Straightening up, the doctor said, "Well, I'll see you in my surgery in five days, just to check you over. It was a hefty knock your head took." Then he turned his attention to Angus.

Mary took a few more items out of her bag. "I couldna find one of your brown sandals. I know they're your favourites, so I brought this wee white pair." For a split second as their eyes met and held, Helen saw the look that flickered across James's face, before he turned away, opening the door for Molly. Helen's heart lifted, then nosedived.

The doctor prepared to go, then, as an afterthought he turned to Mary and Molly. "Ladies, do ye think I ought to maybe wait about a bit?" His eyes twinkled good naturedly. "They do say things happen in threes, you know. Is there anything unexpected likely to happen?" He winked at Angus. The women looked at him in mock horror.

"I know I've been acquiring a little bit of padding, ye canny man, but I'm no expecting a happy event." Molly looked over her shoulder to her friend. "Are you, Mary?" Mary threw up her hands and the two of them went out chuckling like schoolgirls. At the door, they called their good nights, patting James on the arm.

Angus bent and kissed Helen's cheek then crossed the room to where James had been silently watching them. They shook hands with the doctor; as James held the door for him, he said quietly, "I'll bring her to you myself." Pulling the door almost closed, he looked at the precious figure lying in his bed, almost lost in its hugeness.

The room suddenly quiet, a muffled click told her the room was empty. Feeling a sudden sadness and closing her eyes against the now mild throb, she tried to relax. Now almost everything ached. As the bedding enfolded her comfortably, she puzzled as to why James had become rather distant; she supposed he was devastated about the theft of his pedigree stud bull. Five years' work, she had heard someone say. Wondering vaguely if he blamed her in some way for its loss.

Oh, damn you, James McKlinross, damn you and your bull, wherever he is, then she instantly reproached herself. As a small sob escaped her, she turned her face into his pillow trying to picture the new baby in his mother's arms and the proud Andrew. The trauma of the day's happenings had taken their toll; she had been so worried about Ginty and this hadn't been her fault. Helen slipped in and out of a light sleep, waking fully as she realised Stuart was standing at the side of the bed. His face looked strained.

She heard him whisper, "I've come to say goodnight."

Stuart stood motionless gazing down at the figure lying in his brother's bed. He knew a great fondness was developing for this girl that had come to live in the Highlands. Kneeling down and leaning both arms on the bed his face now close to hers, looking straight into her eyes, he felt he could swim in. "How's the bump. It's turning a pretty colour," he said carefully lifting her hair. "I see doc's given you a couple of stitches," then grinning he added, "that's to stop your head falling off, I suppose." Helen couldn't help smiling; he had the same disarming good looks as his brother.

"Are you comfortable; is there anything you'd like me to do for you? If you're a bit bored could do the highland fling." His expression broke into the cheeky grin she was becoming familiar with. Helen laughed silently. He could see why his brother had fallen in a big way; she was rather lovely.

"I'd like to get up for a while, could you turn that comfortable-looking armchair a little towards the window?"

Nimbly getting to his feet as Helen started to push the bedclothes back he said, "Not so hasty my girl, I don't want you falling and have to pick you off the floor for the second time today. Let me move the chair first."

Comfortably settled, Helen pondered his words. So it was Stuart that had carried her in; she vaguely remembered strong arms lifting her. Carefully passing her fingers through her hair in an attempt to encourage it to stay back as he handed her a hairbrush. Looking into his eyes, he had a soft kind side to him she decided. "Thanks, Stuart, for everything."

Voices and soft laughter was coming from the new parents' quarters. In the comfort of the large kitchen, Angus and James chatted as they drank tea. "It's been an unpleasant business for ye, lad, and no mistake." James shrugged looking at his father's old friend and facing him squarely.

"Well I'll not worry about that just now, Angus, both the girls are safe and that's all that matters." Angus could see the strain of the last few hours plainly showing on the young man's face. His strong good looks so like his father. Angus admired him and knew he would always try to do all his own father would have done to help him in any way.

Sighing he said, "Aye that's true enough," and gave him a wry smile. "We have a new wee laddie in the glen, just what the place needs, some new young blood."

James wondered briefly if Angus meant, what he thought he meant. Becoming a little uneasy although the two of them had a strong bond. More than once, he had turned to Angus for guidance, but was Angus aware that Helen may have feelings now for Stuart, or that was his feelings. James knew that he himself loved her with all his being, but she knew her own mind. With a serious note in his voice Angus said, "When she's ready, lad, you'll be seeing to it that she gets home to where she belongs." James inhaled deeply and nodded, but to him, it seemed she was home where she belonged, and he was certainly in no hurry for this lovely girl to leave his bed. She liked the thought of her being in his bed. He knew he was daydreaming. A longing to be near her. "You have my word, Angus."

Mary and Molly went back upstairs to see Helen again and the doctor followed them. James opened his bedroom door for the doctor to do another final check on Helen. Closing the figured wooden door, he leaned against it. Watching the doctor tilt Helen's head back while he looked into her eyes once more, he thought how lovely she was, knowing under the dressing was a nasty gash, feeling his fists clench.

Straightening up, the doctor seemed satisfied for the moment. "Well, I'll see you in my surgery in five days" – putting an envelope on the bedside table – "you can change the dressing in a few days, be careful of the stitches. I'm afraid, my dear, you are going to have some bruising. It's colouring up now. Still never mind, it won't spoil your good looks for long."

Chapter 10

The room was bathed in a soft glow from one bedside table lamp. Sitting looking out of the window, brush in hand, still damp her hair curled into the contours of her cheeks and into her neck, the robe pulled comfortably around her. Helen could see water all around her abruptly remembering she was in the castle. Stars were visible in the velvety blue, and apart from a throbbing headache, she felt calm and peaceful. It was a lovely room with a masculine touch. His room.

Behind her, the door opened and closed quietly. Not really wanting an intrusion into this tranquillity, she sat taking a last look out of the window. James's voice behind her was quiet. "Helen, I've brought someone to see you." Although she didn't feel like seeing anyone at the moment, she turned and smiled, then gasped with delight at the snowy bundle held so carefully in the strong arms, his tanned hands against the shawl, so tender. Lifting her head to look at him and the baby, he saw the bruise and the spiteful cut on her forehead and felt his stomach muscles tighten, his eyes narrowed, and he winced inwardly. He wanted to kiss away the hurt.

Looking at her, with his robe about her body, he wanted to hold her to him. A dark thought clouded his mind as he saw her once again, in his brother's arms kissing his face and whispering to him, was he making a play for her and was she falling for it? Forcing himself to look away, he knelt beside her and leaned so that she could see the baby's pink face and tiny quiff of sandy hair. Mouth slightly open in wonder, she gazed for a long moment at the sleeping baby. "Oh, James, he's a darling." The hairbrush forgotten, along with the headache, she slid to the floor. Smiling, he gently lowered the baby onto her lap, a look of great tenderness on his face.

"Ginty wanted you to see him before you went to sleep."

Looking at each other, she whispered, "Thank you, Uncle James." The corners of his eyes crinkled into a smile. Their faces were very close and his arms were still about the baby. She could feel the hard muscle of his arm against her breast but couldn't trust her elbow to support the precious bundle.

As he made to draw away, then changed his mind, a quiver of delight at the return of contact pulsed through her as he said, "This is truly the work of love."

Leaning forward she whispered, "So perfect and so beautiful."

He turned his head to look at her, his voice husky. "Yes, beautiful." For one mad moment, she wished that she and James had made this baby laying in his arms, and that when she eventually slipped into bed, she would lay in his arms tonight and every night. A small hiccup from the baby brought her back to reality as James lifted the baby from her.

"Is Ginty all right?" He put his head back and chuckled.

"Yes, she said it's the best way to do it, two hours from start to finish." He gave her a sideways look. "Ginty says you and Molly were marvellous, and she doesn't know what she would have done without you." With a wistful look he added, "I missed the important bit." He was going to say something, but let it go.

"Andrew says he's glad her bump is gone." Helen laughed.

"And I've got one…I mean…" she touched her temple, smiling into the smoky depths of his eyes. It was just as well, he mused, that she couldn't read his thoughts.

"How's the head?"

"Fine," she lied. Now that he was getting ready to go, the throbbing was coming back with a vengeance.

On an impulse, she touched his sleeve. "James, I'm sorry about the theft." There was another theft on his mind, and it didn't have four legs. Did she have feelings for his brother Stuart; the girl now puzzled him. Now standing up, she tried to read his expression. "I hope you get him back." James was going to make sure he got back what was his. They moved towards the door as he watched her frame wrapped in his robe. The sleeves hid her hands and the hem trailed on the floor behind her, as the front slightly gapped affording him a view of one of her shapely legs for a few seconds.

At the door, she shook the sleeves back, her fingers on the door handle. James was sitting on the arm of one of the sofas. "What about a goodnight kiss?" his eyes glinted in the dark. Helen held her breath. He made a small movement with his arms, indicating the baby. She came and stood by him, looking down, bending slightly and kissing his head. "He's only four hours old." As she did so,

James saw the curve of her breast then felt the sweet surprise of her lips on his mouth all too briefly.

Slightly embarrassed and not really knowing why she said, "That's for letting me sleep in your bed." Her hands dropped to her sides.

"Helen, you have me at an unfair advantage." His eyes flickered across his robe to his bed.

"Yes, I do." She allowed herself the luxury of fingering his dark hair, then moved to the door.

"This could take some time." He smiled seeing her quizzical expression. "There's my bath, my robe" – he leaned towards her and breathed in – "that's my…" She laughed.

"I also used your toothpaste."

"Well then…" Helen opened the door.

"His mother will be getting anxious."

"Thank you for bringing him to see me; it was lovely of you."

As he passed her in the doorway, he looked appraisingly at her and whispered, "You won't forget you're in my debt." Helen stood in the near darkness for a moment, snapped off the light then crept into his bed pulling his robe around her. Despite her aches, Helen knew she would sleep well tonight.

True to his word, a week later James had delivered Helen to the doctor's, and she had left with a clean bill of health. Now sitting in the lodge kitchen with an attentive audience while she recounted the many cuddles with the new baby. Sighing deeply she said, "Oh, I'm going to miss holding the baby; he's got a real quiff of hair and almost navy blue eyes."

Angus and Mary revelled in the chatter; it was good to have her back. Listening to her, Angus was more than pleased to notice the relaxed way she referred to the new people in her life. "Does your elbow or shoulder hurt you any more, lass?" She smiled at him, the same worried frown on his weather-beaten face.

"I haven't any twinges at all so you can stop worrying, Angus." Getting up to squeeze him around the shoulders and kiss his cheek, then looking more serious she asked, "Did you manage to get to the farmstead with the two little children, almost afraid to ask about the man?"

Mary came bustling forward. "Now we won't go worrying about that, they're all good at the moment and the things you've had delivered to them has nearly had that poor woman beside herself; here's some post." She handed her quite a pile. "David and Lucinder have been in twice to enquire how you were getting on from the Big House." As she started opening the post and standing the get-well cards up, she remembered she was going to ask Angus and Mary about the name of the Big House, on the papers she had it was referred to as the stately home. Smiling at the cards from her brothers and a large one with several names on it from her dance friends telling her perhaps London was safer after all.

Later as they sipped homemade wine, Angus explained that the house was called 'Mount Eagle Place' so called because from the windows of the upper rooms you could watch the magnificent sea eagles circling in the valley and rising on the up winds. "It's a rare sight to be sure." Angus lent towards her and in a quiet voice said, "The family you visited, he's having treatment in hospital and a mite more comfortable, so we will have to wait and see." She smiled gratefully at him.

"Has James mentioned he has to visit one of the islands soon on business?" She felt suddenly excited. "Angus, I'd love to go; he said he might be able to take me with him. I remember Aunt Matty talking about them."

"It's quite a long way, lass, and it can be a rough trip at times, but if you're sure."

Standing on the steps together Angus was staring into the distance; he breathed deeply. "Can ye no smell the wet winds blowing from the isles?" Then pointing he said, "Aye that's real beauty." Helen followed his gaze to where the sharp contrast of mountains was suffused by the sun's glow, the colour so rich no artist could have put it to canvas. Closing her eyes, she locked the memory away as she heard Angus's voice almost a whisper. "The glen holds more secrets than can be learned in a lifetime."

Getting into bed felt a lot different to the castle; her bed was smaller for a start although it was full size, and it seemed strange not hearing water lapping against the stony shore. She was missing saying goodnight to James and the sweet smell of the new baby and her chats with Ginty and James's mother; she had spent hours looking at her photos, the stage sets and costumes had taken her breath away; they certainly spoke the same language. Then when the men had come home galloping into the courtyard and little Duncan squealing with delight at seeing his daddy and watching Andrew pick his son up and cuddle him, then sit him on the saddle and walk to the stables leading him, Helen felt fortunate to feel part of such a lovely family. His wife Ginty was a treasure and they had formed a close friendship.

Chapter 11

This morning, she was feeling comfortably refreshed after a fitful night's sleep disturbed only by a dream that she was searching for her lost sandal, but she wouldn't worry about that now as she had made up her mind to visit two more crofter farms and also call in to the McNeilsons. She was anxious to find out how the father was and the two young children; she would feel happier once she had seen them for herself.

Mary had invited James to dinner; Helen felt her tummy flip at the thought, so she must watch the time. Long shadows chased across green hills, feathery grasses ruffled by the breeze laying them this way and that, she could see deer on the hills every now and then and had stopped for some Galloway cattle, which gave her time to feast on the tapestry that was Scotland.

An avenue of cypresses told her she was here, this looked a little more prosperous, but no one in. The next was tucked into the hillside a grass roof growing, with chickens and a goat walking about on it. At the front, the goat looked down on her; at the back, they all walked straight onto the grassy hillside. After five minutes, Helen decided to give up; there was no response and the goat was getting very noisy and bleating strongly. Thinking she must be upsetting it, she decided to turn around and make tracks for the McNeilsons when suddenly all went quiet, and she heard a woman's voice. "Cend mile failte." A rosy-cheeked lady with a heavy basket on her arm and a feeding bottle with an enormous teat was smiling at her. Helen panicked, as she didn't understand the words she spoke. The woman put the basket down and the bottle holding her arms out to Helen and clasping her. "Cend mile failte" – laughing – "one hundred thousand welcomes, Helen; it's an old Gaelic greeting, ha ha."

An hour later, laden with a sample of her freshly churned butter (and because she had mentioned she had no animals), two baby goats and four chickens, what was Angus going to say. Pulling up at the McNeilson's, her heart lifted. The children were playing and all around looked different.

Bending to see the toy they were showing her, their mother walked over to her looking much improved to the last time she had seen her. There was a faint smile about her lips. She held her hand out. "Helen, how are you, Mrs McNeilson?" The woman clasped her hand.

"Flora and I'm pleased you've come, come in."

The bed had gone from the room and now the children made themselves comfortable on a new sheepskin rug. Helen was relieved to discover that her husband was in a sanatorium in Edinburgh as they had diagnosed him with TB and he was in isolation for the moment but at last responding to the medication. Helen said what good news it was to the children. The older one looked at her and nodded, the younger one got up and leaned towards her mother's face. "But I liked him here, Mummy, where I could see him," he said looking sideways at Helen.

"We will all be going to the hospital soon, and we can talk to him through the glass," then quietly, "we have to be kept an eye on apparently."

"What have you got in the Land Rover, is it a goat?" Helen told them the happenings of the morning; they were soon all laughing.

"And the noise this goat made on the grass roof, well, and its name was Doora on account that it always let her know when someone was at the door; honestly, Flora, I don't know what Angus and Mary will say."

"If you don't want them, we'll have them." The youngest had suddenly brightened up. "Mine's the brown and white one." And he disappeared into the garden.

Looking at her watch, Helen said, "I'm late."

Waving goodbye, Helen was pleased to be relieved of the chickens, goats and butter. Hurrying now as time had moved faster than she had realised. Feeling as if a big worry had left her, she began to hum one of her favourite dance tunes. The allowance had made things a lot easier and rent-free, also the two men who helped out on the small farm during the week had certainly made a big difference, Helen also noticed some repairs had been carried out.

Turning into the lodge, James's car was visible; she sat for a moment knowing she had a collection of hairs and feathers and an offensive odour about her so slipped around the back straight into all three of them.

Looks on their faces made her burst into laughter. Mary was wrinkling her nose looking at James and Angus. "I'm sure there's an explanation; come along indoors, lass and…erm take your shoes off…er."

"It's all right, Mary, I'll tell you all about it." She looked across at James. "Won't be a minute."

"What have you been up to?" he asked raising his eyebrows. Helen showered in double quick time not bothering to dry her hair, skipping happily down the stairs, joined them in the lounge greeting them with 'Cend mile failte'. They looked at each other, surprised. Angus winked at her, then Mary ushered them into dinner. Helen waited until they were all comfortably seated with a drink and she related the day's happenings, smiling widely, proud at remembering the old Gaelic greeting, 'One Hundred Thousand Welcomes', they seemed suitably impressed.

James was looking at her throughout the evening, how lovely she looked; her hair swept back drying naturally and beginning to curl into her neck, eyes bright with enjoyment recalling her day. He lent towards her and lightly kissed her on the cheek smiling at Angus and Mary 'she smells a lot nicer now' letting his fingers slide lightly down her bare arm. "So, Angus, it's all right for me to have the company of Helen next week; we'll be travelling on the 'Snow Goose'. I promise to take good care of her." Too excited to talk, she just smiled. "It'll be for four days. I'll go ahead with the booking in the morning." Mary frowned at Helen.

"Don't you go coming back with any more bumps on the head, lass." Angus sat forward in his chair.

"That reminds me, a policeman was here today who wants to talk to you about the theft of the bull at the castle. Don't look so worried, lass; he's coming at ten o'clock tomorrow." Looking across at James, his expression was unreadable.

Helen was thoughtful. "It might be a good idea to mention a couple of things." Angus was looking at her.

"They're obviously looking for clues, didn't ye say, lass, you would know one of them if he came near you?" She saw James stiffen. Thinking it better to say nothing, she handed around the chocolate mints.

Chapter 12

The Snow Goose rocked gently against the wooden quay, brightly painted and looking pristine for a one hundred years old trawler. Hardly able to contain her excitement, Helen thought she looked like a comfortable old mother hen waiting to gather her charges to her bosom. Looking across at James talking to one of the crew, she was filled with an overwhelming happiness; he looked so handsome and confident. Coming over, he smiled making the back of her knees feel weak and taking her arm saw her safely down the rutted gangplank.

Calm water made the crossing of the loch enjoyable. "Happy?" he asked looking directly into her eyes as he held her around the waist.

"Very," she replied laughing as he gave her a discreet squeeze.

"The Isle of Fay is about two hours away, we should make good time." As they neared the narrow fissure with its towering rocks, Norse Mountain one side and Split rock on the other leading them into the Atlantic Ocean, conditions suddenly changed. Helen leaned into James, a question in her look as a deafening roaring ahead of them took her by surprise. "It's all right, look we are at sea now."

Leaving behind the shelter of the mountains now in the open sea, the waves were crashing against the rocks along the coast; they seemed to be bouncing about as the old trawler headed bravely into the wind. An hour later, the conditions were very rough to Helen's way of thinking, feeling the cold seeping into her, holding onto the side it was getting difficult to stay upright. James took her white-knuckled hands from the rail and firmly escorted her into the large cabin. There were only twelve passengers who all seemed to know each other, and James chatted comfortably to them as he put a steaming cup of hot chocolate into Helen's hands and steadied her, grinning as he introduced her as 'my lady'. Through the spray-spattered window could be seen an emerald green necklace of islands resting serenely in the distance as Snow Goose cut through the water; it was magical.

A shout from the helm, James went with a few other men out on deck; it appeared there was a well charted dangerously strong whirlpool as they neared the island; they had obviously done this before. The wheel had to be wrestled hard over to stay well away from the danger spot. Now she could feel the pull and for the first time was frightened watching the giant circles spinning and the dark centre dipping menacingly and the men leaning their weight together on the large wheel keeping it from spinning towards the circles. Once clear, they all breathed a sigh of relief shaking hands with each other.

Putting his arms completely around her, looking at her upturned face, he kissed her nose as they watched the island come nearer. His face showed sheer pleasure as he pointed to another boat coming in at the same time, boxes of lobsters could be plainly seen. Looking at his handsome profile, his dark hair curling onto his forehead with the damp air, dark brows and lashes, strong straight nose, lips in a ready smile and clean cut jawline was something Helen could feast on. Suddenly bending his head towards her he said, "I hope you like your stay. I will enjoy having you all to myself." The smile held promise. Helen slipped her arms inside his coat and laid her head against his heart as he pulled her to him.

"I will like my stay because I'm here with you." The look that passed between them said more than any words could say.

Snuggling her comfortably under his arm with a look of sheer pleasure, they watched the colourful fishing boats jostling in the harbour, the bare-chested men unloading the lobster crates that had pulled in almost alongside them. Safely on dry land, walking along the jetty, the little stone and wooden houses fronting a road of well-worn stones surprised her. He was pointing to a large building with a swinging sign that said 'Sentinel'. James informed her that was where they would be staying. It looked very old and full of history noticing the comfortable looking well-worn wooden seats dotted around outside. Inside although a bit primitive had a warm peat and log fire and some tempting aromas.

James was treated like a long lost friend. After a filling dinner of baked fish, crusty bread, potatoes grown in peat and oatcakes, Helen felt too full to move. Turning to James dabbing her mouth with the serviette, she said, "Shall we go for a walk, the beach looked quite good."

"Have you had enough to eat?" he asked passing the plate of cakes to her. She tapped her tummy and shook her head.

The tide was going out and the beach was flat with surprising golden sand any holiday resort would have been proud of. "This is normal for Scotland." He saw her bend and pick up a handful of sand.

"Do you know, all the years we came to Aunt Matty—" She stopped as saying her name brought memories swimming before her. Swallowing hard, she looked at the skyline. "We never bothered to go to the seaside; we had all we needed." He stroked her hair letting his fingers touch the softness of her cheek. His feelings ran deep, and he had to wrestle with himself.

Curling his fingers into hers, he said, "Come on, let's run our dinner off."

Laughing and puffing, they stopped at a small cave entrance deciding to explore it. "You can see how rough the sea can get." Yes, she could; the cave was piled high at one end with boulders and stones flung there by the incoming tide and the floor of the cave looked like a cobbled floor laid by hand; she walked carefully over it as a large crab scuttled across. "Go and hide or the lobster man will get you. Er, isn't this where you are supposed to jump into my arms?" She looked at him and saw mischief in his face.

"Perhaps if it were about four times bigger—" she was not being able to finish as James took her gently in his arms.

"I'll look for one." Then he turned her to him. "I've been wanting to do this all day," he said kissing her gently on the mouth at first, then letting his passion surface.

They walked back along the sand. "You know, Helen, I might not take you home; I might run away with you." He stopped abruptly. Coming around to stand in front of him, he was smiling, feeling her heart miss a beat, the same way it did at their meeting by the burn; she reached up and cupped his face in her hands; she loved this man and would readily run away with him knowing they were both daydreaming.

On tiptoes, she just about managed to reach his lower chin and kissed him whispering, "You'll have to catch me first," and turned and started running up the beach, laughing.

Seconds later, she was scooped up in his arms laying back grinning. Feelings he had for this lovely girl were beyond any he'd experienced before, her chestnut hair lay over his arm, the laughing eyes that spoke to him without her knowing, the sweet mouth that he dreamed nightly about kissing, her heart-shaped face and slender neck remembering the way she danced for him all those years ago, hardly being able to believe she was here in his arms. How he thanked the dead deer hanging under the waterfall, then he had held her so tenderly as she cried in his arms, but they had been children, now he was a man and knew he was going to have to get to grips with himself.

Lowering her to the sand, he said, "And where do you think you were going?" They were standing looking at one another.

"I was going to get my things, you did say – I might run away with you…" Looking at her for a long moment, he sighed. "What am I going to do with you? That reminds me, I'll call in at the garage by the quay. I want to see if Blondie is free." Helen had a little sinking feeling, as the last moments of magic were gone.

Studying this very old white rough terrain vehicle, she wondered if it would even go, but James was arranging for her to have it at her disposal tomorrow. "You will be able to see a little bit of the island in Blondie; she is a sturdy little run about. I will be tied up all day, but we'll hopefully have the evening together." The thought occurred to her that her feet might not reach the pedals, but she would worry about that tomorrow.

Back in the pub-cum-hotel, they made their way to their rooms stopping outside Helen's; she told James she was going to wash and change and would see him in the bar. A little later, she descended the stairs to see James already comfortable in an armchair with a drink, looking relaxed.

The locals were very friendly, asking her lots of questions and suggest following the coast road tomorrow with Blondie; she told them she wanted to photograph some of the beauty spots and had brought her aunt's binoculars. An elderly local, Dougal, made her laugh and the farmer's son Hamish told her 'cattle and sheep sometimes wander onto road mind'.

Before turning in for the night, James took Helen onto the front courtyard of the pub. They stood breathing in the night air, marvelling at the view before them. The evening light was fading; in the distance, a white gauze veil of mist hung low, delicate as gossamer. Tops of hills pushed through the mist giving them an eerie feel. Looking the other way, rugged peaks of the highlands sloping away to misty green beauty of the lowlands. Helen turned to James sweeping her hand across the vista. "I'm going to take this to bed with me." He caught her hand and lifted it to his lips. "Sweet dreams, my love."

In her room, Helen looked at her hand; her dreams would be sweet indeed. Drawing the curtains, she could hear the waves breaking on the beach and knew the tide was well in, and she was getting excited about tomorrow. A couple of the locals had offered to escort her around the island, but she had graciously declined.

The next thing she knew was she could hear a tapping on the door.

"Tea, Miss Helen. I'll leave it out hear." She rubbed her eyes and wondered what time it was.

"Thank you, that's fine." *James must have ordered early morning tea; he said he had an early start.* Then she groaned as her watch said 8.30 am. Outside in the hall way was tea on a tray and a very large jug of hot water. Looking out of the window at the comings and goings of the bustling little port, she suddenly saw James. An impressive car had just pulled up by him. He looked up at the window. Easing the quaint old metal framework of the window to move, Helen managed to get the reluctant window to open; she leaned out and blew him a kiss. He saw her and waved, then got in the car and was gone.

Chapter 13

The dining room was deserted. She helped herself to scrambled egg and round fried potatoes; the man from behind the bar from the night before brought her a pot of tea. "You be off with Blondie, lass." He poured the tea for her. "Be sure to stay on the good road ye al be all right then, lass. Blondie, erl look after ee, don't go strayin."

Collecting the rough terrain vehicle, Helen started off straight away armed with a map, her camera and binoculars, a small picnic, as she didn't plan to stay out all day. A stiff breeze off the sea made map reading difficult if not impossible, but it had looked quite straightforward.

Blondie was an absolute joy; she purred along comfortably and was easy to drive. The coast road was rough in places with breath-taking scenery to compensate. Passing many lovely places that she wanted to catch on camera, stopping several times and pleased with her efforts capturing a stunning view of a golden stretch of sandy coastline with rugged cliffs and three colours of green and blue in the sea. Deciding to push on and capture some other beauty spots on the way back.

Later, checking her watch, she decided it was time for lunch and pulled into a quaint little halt. Not remembering seeing anything about a railway, she chose a wooden bench and enjoyed her rolls of thinly cut meat, a napkin with buttered oatcake and dates and a nobly piece of cheese. Satisfied, she put her head back and looked at the sky full of broken cloud allowing a small amount of blue through and low white puffball clouds over the sea, wondering what James was doing at the moment. Closing her eyes, she listened to the sea's rhythmic motion and the crying of the gulls, becoming aware of another noise gradually getting louder, smiling as she saw a train approaching.

James sat at a table perusing maps. He was part of a team that were planning an observatory as the one in use now had too much light pollution and the island and inky black nights seemed a perfect location. Wondering how Helen was getting on with Blondie, perhaps he had been a bit hasty in wanting her to see the island thinking now it might have been better to wait for him. A booming voice interrupted his thoughts. "Mr McKlinross, we would like your thoughts on location and bearings." James stood up.

Watching the hill train announce its approach with squeals and groans and much wheezing, as it came panting by, Helen could almost feel it gearing itself up to take the next steep incline ahead. Amused, it occurred to her that a dedicated jogger, had there been one on the island, could have quite easily outpaced it.

Feeling the breeze picking up a little stronger now, she slipped on her jacket, hearing Angus's words in her head; it's the moist Atlantic air streams breathing over the mountains. Smiling to herself, she turned Blondie, hesitating a few moments watching the curlews and gulls and some boats a long way out, but she could see them clearly through the binoculars and felt pleased with herself for catching a guillemot surfacing with a fish with her camera.

Meeting hardly any other traffic except a few tractors and an old school bus with a handful of children in it that called out to Blondie, she drove on feeling happy about her day out when she saw the spot she had been looking for, pulling in and parking at the edge of the road. It was beautiful; the hill sloped away from her with an emerald green dip that rolled up the other side looking like velvet as it met the sky. The sun was beginning to get low and the light would soon fade. Taking the remains of lunch, which was a chocolate bar and a small apple and a couple of boiled sweets, and hanging her camera and binoculars around her neck, she set off up the first hill. The hollow was set between two sweeping hills and she tackled this next. The view from up here was wonderful. Sitting on a flat boulder with her back against a rock, she ate her chocolate. Blondie was now a speck in the distance, but the road could be clearly seen. There were a few clouds now; she wasn't worried.

Leaning sideways to take a snap of the contours of the hill, she moved her position to lean further out feeling she was sitting on something. Running her hand through the gravely grass, she felt something half buried, pulling it out saw it was a clay pipe. Turning it over, she decided it was no ordinary pipe and must have been lovingly made by a shepherd.

Slipping the pipe into her picnic bag, she noticed the sun had almost gone just as some sheep came over the rise. Helen gasped at the sight before her; the colours were magic. As the sun dropped below the hill, a saffron band lay along the ridge giving them a golden crest catching the backs of the sheep turning their fleece a burnished bronze against an emerald background. Helen was excited, what a picture this would make and hurriedly climbed a bit higher knowing she would get some beautiful photos.

An hour later, she was satisfied she had all she wanted, going over the top of the hill had found highland cattle with the same golden hue on their backs highlighting their ginger brown colouring with the purple shades of evening on the far mountains. A little further down, she could see what she knew to be Clydesdales, two heavy working horses, their mains flowing in the breeze. Feeling elated with her collection of photos, she started the long climb back. The hill was a steep climb, and she was getting tired, jumping a gully suddenly aware she hadn't done that before. Studying the landscape, she decided to go on. Fifteen minutes later, she knew this wasn't the way and felt the first pangs of fear. *Now come on, Helen, the road is over that hill somewhere*; she stopped and popped a boiled sweet in her mouth. *What am I going to tell them? Oh, hallo, I'm back, but I've lost Blondie.* Turning around, she began to retrace her footsteps feeling real fear now as the light was fading fast. Thinking she had let them down hadn't they warned her to stay on the good road.

Her lip quivered, and she rummaged for a hankie. It was then she saw the dog, standing on a hill above her. She wiped her eyes. *I'm not going to cry, it's my own fault, everywhere looks the same.* She called to the dog, "Are you lost too?" The dog didn't move. Adjusting the camera on her shoulder as it was all becoming uncomfortable, she noticed the dog had gone. Feeling angry with herself for not taking more notice of the path she had taken, she sat for a moment on low rock deciding she was going to keep climbing upwards. The dog was on the next rise. Helen climbed towards it talking to it. It stood motionless watching her as she took its photo adjusting the light. "I hope your photograph comes out." It was quite a pretty slightly built white dog with largish pointed ears. Putting the camera lens cover on and slipping it over her shoulder, she saw the dog was gone.

It was quite dark now, and she couldn't pretend she wasn't really scared, shaking slightly, she knew she was near the top of the rise and going over could just make out the thin ribbon of road a long way below but no sign of Blondie, but she could see the dog again standing on a ledge watching her; she called to it feeling in need of its company. Putting her head in her hands, she groaned. From somewhere nearby, she heard her name being called. "Oh, no, not a talking dog; am I having delusions like they do in the desert?" Taking her hands from her eyes, she saw a long way below her a flashlight and heard her name called again. Scrambling down the slope, her heart was thumping. "Are you looking for me?"

The light flashed and a voice called, "It's me, Miss Helen, Hamish."

It was a long walk down to the road. Hamish smiled knowingly at her as he sat her on the back of his motorbike and drove to where Blondie was parked, and Helen realised she had been going in the wrong direct, but she had told Hamish excitedly about the photos, and she did get disorientated and showed him the clay pipe and told him about the white dog, and no, the dog wasn't lost. He lifted his motorbike effortlessly into the back of Blondie and drove them both back.

At the Sentinel, Hamish offered to take Blondie back to the garage for her as the car with James in had just pulled up. He looked tired. James kissed her gently on the mouth telling her she was the best thing he'd seen today.

Looking at the back of Hamish returning Blondie, she had a similar feeling.

He put his briefcase in the doorway. "Let's just take a few steps on the beach," Not waiting for her answer and guiding her by her elbow, they were soon almost to the waterline. He stood breathing deeply as he gazed out to sea. Helen wondered if his day had been stressful, thinking he would tell her eventually, but looking at him now he was smiling.

"It seems to have been a long day waiting to be back with you, my darling." He clasped her around the waist. She smiled up at him. "Is that your tummy I can hear rumbling?" Taking her hand, they walked back across the beach, immediately into the smell of dinner. Running up the stairs and laughing because Helen beat him, they arranged to meet in the dining room.

In her room, she changed in double quick time. There was so much she had to tell him and lots of questions also. Tomorrow, when she collected Blondie, she would be more careful where she went walking and not wander across the hills, well, not too far. Feeling excited at the freedom of driving herself about, skipping down the stairs, she saw James already at the table.

Chapter 14

Relaxing in front of a glowing peat fire with a few sticks of pine giving a pleasant aroma, Helen studied James's face as reflections from the fire lit his eyes and momentary flashes of white as he spoke. Dinner had been venison reminding her of the waterfall when they were young, and she found it hard to enjoy taking only a little, but the rest was tasty.

Cock a Leekie soup, the spices just right and all the trimmings from the roast, onions, carrots, celery, red wine and it had been braised with cranberries and red currant jelly, Helen's favourite. In the centre of the table had been the largest Dundee cake, heavy with blanched almonds she had ever seen, knowing her slice was too big but she was unable to say no.

Dougal and Hamish were in the bar talking about the clay pipe she had found, and as the evening went on, interest in the pipe grew. Finding it hard to tell James about her day as he was very popular and in demand, she sat back enjoying the fire and accented mix of voices. From across the bar, she noticed Dougal beckoning her, patting a chair alongside him.

Introducing her to an auburn haired – mainly on his chin – gentleman who was turning the clay pipe over in his large hands that also had auburn hair on them Helen noticed. Passing Hamish, she put her hand on his shoulder and whispered 'my hero' causing him to blush deeply and the man next to him to nudge him as she sat in the chair Dougal indicated, and she smiled across at James, who was now watching her with interest.

The green eyes with gold flecks in a ruddy face looked at her for a long moment as if he were trying to read her mind. Dougal nodded his head. "Bruce here wants to ask you about the pipe, lass."

Describing as best she could and offering to show anyone interested where she had found it, tomorrow if they wished and finding her audience growing as the evening went on. With her face radiating excitement she said, "I can't wait to get my photos developed, the landscape higher up is wonderful, the views out to sea and scenery." Looking at the interested faces around her, she was beginning to feel quite important. One of the onlookers wanted to know what else she could see while up there.

"Clydesdale horses over the ridge in the sunset, and the sheep coming over the top with the sun on their backs turning their wool orange gold." Now feeling a little shy, she looked down at her hands. "I hope the one with the lovely white dog comes out." A hush, as they looked towards each other then back at Helen. Bruce handed back the clay pipe, a glint in his eyes.

"A white dog you say?" A whisper went around. "Can you tell us more, lass, where exactly did you see this white dog?"

Helen felt them visibly lean forward. "It was when…when I thought I was lost. I was trying to make my way back to where I'd parked Blondie." A gentle laughter pervaded. "I was getting tired and I sat down for a moment, that's when I first saw the dog, a little higher up. I called to it, but it didn't move." A few more whispers. "I carried on over the top, but it had gone. Do you know the dog; is it lost?"

"Eye, we know the dog and no, she isn't lost."

Helen felt a wave of relief; there had been something about the dog, but she couldn't put her finger on it. Looking at their expectant faces, they were waiting to hear more, so Helen smiled and carried on. "The next time I saw her was when I knew I was on the right path for the road." She hadn't meant to say that.

"Did you lose your way a little, Helen?" Dougal's eyes were wide with interest.

"…Just a bit, but when I walked to where the dog was, she was gone, but I could see the road so I knew it was okay. I didn't see her anymore." The room filled with excited chatter. Dougal picked up the pipe and handed it to Bruce again.

"Aye, I know this is McTavish's pipe, all right." Turning to Helen, Bruce raised his eyebrows. "What you saw, my dear, was McTavish's spirit dog, Lilly." Letting out a long breath, he continued, "That dear sweet dog never stopped looking for him after he went missing." Feeling in his pocket, he brought out his own pipe, almost the same. "We sat together when we made these; it was a long time ago. I wasn't more than a laddie." He pointed to the initials almost smoothed over now and put it alongside his own pipe.

Helen felt a few questions burning inside her. "How long has Mr McTavish been missing?" Dougal drained his glass and put it down heavily.

"Aw about thirty years."

She felt the hairs on her arms stand up as James put a drink into her hand. "I think I've said this before to you; I can't take my eyes off you for a moment. You do get yourself in deep water." They smiled at each other remembering a certain waterfall when he had said the same words to her.

Back in front of the fire. "Don't read too much into it, Helen darling, it's an old story."

Turning large questioning eyes towards him, she said, "But I did see a white dog, James." Sipping her drink, she was thoughtful. "When I get the photos developed, you'll see."

He pointedly said, "That might not be possible, dear." She looked into James's eyes with realisation that there would be only greenery on the photos that she thought she had taken of the dog. If it were true that what she had seen was a spirit dog, then when she looked at the empty photo, she would imagine her there, not completely trusting that she wouldn't be; she would have to wait and see.

As the people in the bar settled down and chatter was back to normal, they both sat back around the fire, now dying embers but still giving out heat. "I've told the garage you won't be needing Blondie tomorrow." Feeling slight disappointment, she frowned at him.

"Blondie and I got on very well. I enjoyed driving her; we went as far as the railway halt; there was a little shop there." But someone was speaking to him, so it was left there.

Chapter 15

"Tomorrow as long as it's all right with you, Dougal is going to accompany you." He gently brushed a wayward lock of hair, seeing for a second the fading small scar, jolting his memory back. Sliding his arm around her, he gently squeezed. "You are precious." He took a deep breath and looked at the darkening sky at the window. "I only wish we could spend tomorrow together." Looking at his forlorn expression, she slipped her hand into his just as the man from behind the bar came with two cups of coffee with creamy bubbles swirling around the top.

"Thanks, Andy." James reached for his pocket.

"Oh, no, lad, the wee lass has been a might entertaining, there no interested in goin home yet." Smiling, he winked at Helen and went back behind the bar.

Looking around, she could see the interested chatter and the locals did seem a bit more lively and were still passing the clay pipe around. The coffee was delicious due no doubt to the 'wee dram' it had been doctored with and not so little. Feeling the effect of the long day and warm fire and coffee, Helen could hardly keep her eyes open telling James, as she rubbed her eyes, that the sand man was coming. As they got up to go, Dougal came over handing the clay pipe to her; his cheeks were red and his eyes twinkled in his old face, rubbing his hands together he said, "It's a long time since I had a date with a beautiful young lady. I'll be here after breakfast, James." Putting his cap on and touching it, he called goodnight to his friends, and at the door, he stood looking into the night. "Aw, it's a braw brie moonlit nic to nic." Then he was gone.

They made their way upstairs pausing in Helen's room for a lingering kiss; he felt passionate as he caressed her shapely body, kissing her eyes, mouth and neck and looking longingly at the bed. He bade her goodnight.

Dreamily pulling on her brushed cotton plaid pyjamas and teasing the stubborn window open, she leaned into the night. The air came in a gust of coldness, and she breathed it in. The sea seemed to be thundering, heaving and hissing onto the beach, as pebbles rolled back into the waves.

James went slowly into his room, closed the door and leaned against it. He longed for the time when they could be together, not like this with a wall between them. There was nothing he could do until this rustling was sorted out; it bothered him, but sometimes he found it very hard to keep control. Knowing he was too wide awake now to sleep, he went back to the bar lounge for a couple of hours.

Laying comfortably in her cosy plaids, she listened to the sea; there seemed to be no stars tonight. Pulling the bedclothes over her, she lay thinking of the happenings of the evening; she had washed the clay pipe, and it was almost white now; popping it into the pocket of the dressing gown provided by the pub landlord, she laid it across the small bed. Within minutes, she drifted into a fitful sleep.

There were only a handful of people in the bar now, and James was in conversation with the barman and two locals, and he was asking if they had any problems with cattle or sheep rustling on the island, but they had not heard of any, but one of them knew some cattle had been brought in recently, but that was normal for those that wanted to introduce new blood into their herds. "Now I'm takin bets that Dougal turns up tomorrow in his best tweeds and trilby." He produced a notepad and pencil; the men were rummaging in their pockets, but James declined; there was already a list of names saying what he would wear. The barman elaborated on the subject of Dougal's clothes, "You see, his uncle in New Zealand left all his clothes to him and him being a golfer." They all broke out in laughter. "There were mountains of them; half the island are walking about in them. When he went to the mainland to collect the parcels, they nigh on filled the boat, talk about one size fits all." Another peal of laughter.

On a more serious note, James told them about the theft of his prize bull Out of the Blue and how serious the rustling was getting, warning them.

Helen woke with a start; she was sure she heard a dog bark, lying motionless, listening but all was quiet, then out of the corner of her eye, she was sure she saw the dressing gown laid across the bed, move. Pulling the covers over her face, she felt herself breaking out in a cold sweat. Afraid almost to move, lowering the sheet with shaking hands, she could see a small part of the dressing gown start to lift slowly as shadows in the corners of the room seem to materialise. Lying rigid with fear, suddenly able to get her legs to move, literally flew out of the room.

In James's room, dropping to the floor on her knees beside his bed trying not to scream. "James, wake up," she said looking back over her shoulder.

Raising himself up on his elbow, James asked, "Helen, what's the matter?"

"…In there in there…it's a ghost." He smiled.

"You've just had a dream, go back to bed."

"I can't…I can't, James. I'm frightened." Standing up, she stared at the door. "I tell you it's a ghost." Panting. "It moved across the other bed and started to make the clothes rise up getting bigger. I'm frightened."

James looked at her and smiled, pulling the bedclothes back and indicating with his head. "Come on, jump in."

Helen slid gingerly in alongside him and cuddled into him shivering in spite of her cosy plaid pyjamas. "A ghost you say, I must remember to thank him. This is an unexpected pleasure." Smiling broadly, he put his arm around her kissing her ear and whispering, "You know you're making a habit of this." She looked at him pleadingly.

"I'm not going back in there." He could see now that she really was frightened, and she was shivering. Pulling the covers up over them both, he snuggled her into him. Helen could feel the warmth filter into her; she fitted perfectly to the contours of his body.

"You say the bedding rose up slowly?"

"Yes…no…it was the dressing gown, really scary…it sort of started to rise up." He knew exactly what she meant; having her at this unexpected close proximity, he was experiencing the same feeling.

"Are you sure you didn't have a bad dream, what exactly woke you up?"

"It was a dog barking." Helen sat up "James! You haven't…any clothes on." He sighed.

"No, I don't wear clothes in bed." He slid his arm out to reach some clothing. "You took me by surprise, there, better. Go to sleep."

He snapped the light off. Stroking her shoulder gently, he closed his eyes knowing he was walking on a tight rope.

Laying reassuringly alongside him and letting her head sink into the pillow, Helen tried to relax and let her mind drift to the photos she had taken. As soon as they were home, she would take them to be developed. Suddenly remembering the photo of the lone bull a long way off in the depth of a deep valley.

Half turning. "Something else, James."

"Go to sleep."

"But it was something I took a photo of when I was at the top of…"

"Helen, I've a busy day tomorrow, go to sleep, darling." Her eyes were turned towards him with moonlight shining in them; he knew her cheeks were flushed. The neat nose he loved to kiss was inches from him and the lovely mouth that tantalised him was slightly open invitingly. He closed his eyes and prayed for guidance. Turning into her pillow again, she decided to tell him about the bull another time, thinking it was probably of no importance. Feeling safe with his arm around her, she was soon asleep.

Wide awake now and looking at the way her hair lay in folds on the pillow, he listened to her breathing, aware of her warm body lying closely to his. Knowing she was well asleep, he slipped out of bed gently covering her shoulders. Standing in front of the window, the moon was lighting the edge of the waves that were coming in with some force.

Stretching his arms up and running his hands through his hair, feeling the powerful ache in his thighs, he groaned whispering under his breath, "Helen, Helen, what have you done to me?" Knowing he wouldn't last the night in the same bed and thinking reluctantly he would go into her room, he quietly went out of the door. He wouldn't take her here like this; there would be another time and place; he pulled the door closed. The hallway was dimly lit, and he started towards her room. He stood still, the hairs on the back of his neck rising as he felt a figure behind him. Turning, he jumped then saw it was Sandy the owner,

"Number 12 wants em" – indicating the pillows under his arm – "you look as though you've seen a ghost, lad, got a pot of coffee brewing."

"I'll just get a dressing gown."

At breakfast, the topic of conversation had been Helen's 'visitor'. In spite of this, she had experienced a restful night's sleep. They had breakfasted together, and Helen felt calm and rested, as for tonight, she would have to wait and see…

The barman was clutching some paper and looking out of the door, but Dougal hadn't appeared along the road yet and tension was mounting as to what he would be wearing for today's outing with Helen. There were whispers already, and the barman had predicted a full bar tonight.

Before breakfast, they had walked along the shoreline-watching fishermen manhandle their boats up the beach, then divide the catch into piles. James had told her it was between families and how they helped each other out. They had stood watching curlew on the tide, gulls and boats on hold until hunger had driven then in. Now they were both tucking into boiled kippers swimming in butter, then toast with whisky marmalade and a fresh pot of coffee. A commotion at the door made all those in the dining room look and a cheer went up as Dougal entered wearing a smart pair of golfing tweeds, a well cut jacket with a yellow waistcoat and chocolate shirt holding a cap under his arm. "We're gonna have some fun tonight, Dougal, when I read out the 'winner'."

"No winners unless they get me boots right on that there bit o paper." And with that, he stretched one foot out showing the diamond-patterned colourful golfing sock and a spiked shoe. Helen thought the chequered breeches something else.

There was a telephone call for Helen. "Is it a male or female caller?" She was immediately fearful something was wrong at the lodge.

"It's a call from the mainland, Miss Glenkerry, a man's voice." The phone was handed over to her. Her hand shook.

"Hallo, is that you, Angus?" There was laughter at the other end of the phone, and she was relieved if not puzzled to hear Stuart's voice.

"It's me, sweetie, wondered how you were getting on with that brother of mine." Taken aback for a moment, she didn't answer straight away. "We are all missing you; I'm missing you." There was a pause. "I hope he's behaving himself with a lovely girl like you."

"James is working hard, but I'm enjoying myself. I think the island of Fay is delightful and the people are so friendly; in fact, two of the locals are taking me out today. Is every one all right back there, is the baby okay?" Thinking it best to keep the conversation short and not to encourage Stuart. "My escorts have just arrived, Stuart, thank you for the call." And she replaced the receiver hurriedly turning to see James a little way from her and not liking his expression. Giving him a wide smile she said, "That gave me a scare. I thought something was wrong at the lodge." He didn't respond and the expression remained. "It's only Stuart being Stuart." And slipping her arm in his, they went into the fresh air.

Dougal appeared. "Have you no coat, lass, it can get a might breezy." Helen went in running up the stairs to collect her things, camera, binoculars, coat and hurried back down worried that James would have been collected before she got back, but he was there chatting to Dougal; she caught the last few words.

"I'm trusting you to stay with her."

"There's nobody better, James lad, oh, has she got her walking shoes on?" All looking at Helen's feet drew a chuckle.

Going in the opposite direction to yesterday, a little way along the stony road and surprised to see a lighthouse set among the rocks above the beach, she undid her camera and snapped the lighthouse. Noticing a small shop, she bought some sweets and chocolate and a book on the Island of Fay. Looking at her change saw some coins she didn't recognise but dropped them into her purse thinking the island may have its own currency. Dougal was a little way ahead of her now and singing happily; she strained to catch the words. "In the bonnie land of heather, they brewed a drink lang syne, twas sweeter far than honey, and stronger still than wine."

Helen felt very happy to be out with Dougal; they were walking the coast road with a fine view of the neighbouring islands, and he was telling her about the history. "We highlanders are a mixture, especially on the islands, North Sea Rovers, mysterious Picks, Celtic settlers. Of course, it's peaceful now, but we have a turbulent history, lass." Stopping, he lit his pipe and looked out across the water. The rippled sand stretched to the water reflecting the sky, the wild isolated beauty held a haunting attraction. Letting her gaze scan die rolling contours of the hills and valleys and drinking in the peace and solitude, she felt a warm contentment. Dougal was watching her. "You all no see the dog Lilly today?" He was smiling. "Your no lost." They started walking again, and Helen ventured to ask where they were going. "A man who knows where he is going, never asks the way." He looked across at her. "That's an old proverb."

"Yes, but where are you taking me?" They had been walking for an hour, and there were some whitewashed houses coming into view. He stopped and knocked his pipe out gently on the heel of his shoe.

"Just up here we can go down a cut in and visit my friend's farm." Fifteen minutes later, they were walking up the farm driveway, and Helen recognised the motorbike alongside a shed. The surroundings were well kept but poor. A young woman appeared at the door looking surprised. "I've brought a wee visitor to see you, Megan."

After an enjoyable drink, twin boys the image of Hamish took her to find him in one of the barns, but not being able to run him to ground, they took her into their play shed and showed her their precious collection of coins. Shaking her purse out, the loose coins matched theirs. "But I don't recognise this money." And the children started giggling. "It's Spanish money; there was a Scandinavian ship that floundered on the rocks." The two excited faces told her the story of how the cargo was so light it floated ashore. "Beeswax and olive oil and all this money, you get it in your change sometimes." Helen was intrigued but began to wonder about Dougal. "Oh, he'll be having a wee dram, let's go and find Dad."

As they all emerged from the play shed, Hamish was coming across the yard and the children ran to him, and he ruffled their hair, greeting Helen he introduced the boys to her Bruce and Jock.

"They are a credit to you and your wife, and I've been entertained by them. I know all about the ship that went down."

"Daddy the lady gave us her Spanish money; she didn't want it." The boys started to laugh. "Called it funny money." Megan had done some baking and set them on their way with a bag with four cakes. Dougal was in fine song as they started back and Helen thought he must have had more than a wee dram.

"Helen, did ye learn about Mary Queen of Scots at school?"

The question took her by surprise, suddenly remembering the picture on the wall in the Sentinel. Searching her memory, smiling as Dougal was still singing she said, "…Er, didn't she do something awful to the guardian of Inverness Castle?" She hoped this would convince him.

Taking a long draw on his pipe he replied, "Mmm, yes, you mean when he wouldn't let her in." His face took on a strange expression. "Yes, well, that was positively the last time we Scots were inhospitable to visitors." Looking at his pipe, he started to knock its contents out on the heel of his shoe. Thoughtful, pointing the empty pipe to the hills. "Twas Mary who named the famous…castle, aye, that's right; it's said she looked upon the kingdom, saying quel beau lieu."

"They didn't teach me that in school, what does it mean?" His face broke into a warm smile, spreading his arms. "What a beautiful place." Looking at each other, the smiles broke into laughter.

"Aye, the bonnie woman didna lie, tis tranquil now." Then in his strong Scottish brogue he said, "The bens and glens have seen more than their share of clan bloodshed. I tell ye, lass, when the savage winds blow, it's almost as though those plaid clad men of the past are wreaking vengeance." They started to walk towards the tide line. "This here is still called Rebel Beach." Helen bent down and collected a few shells.

Walking on the firm sand still amazed at the pristine beach, deciding to ask Dougal what the unpleasant smell was in the air.. He pointed in the distance. "They are peat cutters away up there and laying it to dry in the wind, see the whitewashed farmhouse, well, that's the distillery." Helen felt sure that they were now headed in its direction. Dougal took a deep breath. "That's why our whisky is unique; its distinct flavour is because of our peat water, where else in the world would you get these conditions?" He was looking out to sea. "You must follow your dram, lass…I mean dream."

Shaking her hair back from her face and running her fingers through her windswept hair, she studied the contours of the hilly landscape. With the waves rhythmically breaking behind her, a feeling of contentment gradually spread over her. With Dougal singing happily to himself in the background, she let her mind wander to James, picturing him studying large maps of the Island of Fay.

"Ye'll no see Lilly now, lass, no, see, you're not lost anymore."

Suddenly coming back to the present, she smiled at him. "I wasn't looking for the dog." Not realising she had been putting the binoculars to her eyes. "I was just wondering where the new observatory might be built. James said something about a bowl I think."

"Ah…that…will probably be Faybles Basin." He came and stood closer to her. "Ya'll be surprised to know, lass, that it's told millions of years ago" – speaking with great enthusiasm – "a mighty meteorite collided with our island – boom – and left the basin-shaped lowlands. Aye, there's nairn like em anywhere else."

Dougal looked at her strangely. Slipping into his exaggerated storytelling dialect. "Do ye know there are some folks that say, while he was enjoying his pipe on his favourite outcrop up there McTavish was taken off the hills by a spaceship." They both lapsed into thought, looking at the hills. "Funny how McKlinross is talking about an observatory to look at the stars and planets." He began to get his pipe out. Helen felt a slight discomfort.

"Can we get a coffee or something before we go any further?"

Dougal was full of apologies. "Will ye forgive me – forgetting me manners." A short walk up onto the road soon found them sitting comfortably in 'Shoreside Refreshments' looking for all the world to Helen like someone's front room but very comfortable. The lady of the house was cheerful and friendly taking Helen by surprise by already knowing her name and obviously being in charge of all tasks. The coffee was good and the plate of shortbread biscuits sweet and more-ish. Views from the window were clear and uninterrupted to the hazy skyline.

"How long are you keeping this wee girl out, Dougal? The clouds are gathering on the horizon."

"Och, away with ye, we're not in any hurry."

The observatory team were taking a break and a neat tall redheaded young woman was talking avidly to James and touching his arm every now and again.

She flashed him a warm intimate smile. "It's good to see you, James." She looked down coyly giving full advantage of her long eyelashes. "It's been a long time; I suppose you don't get to Edinburgh much now." She smiled fully into his face. "Still, we will have to meet and catch up." She tugged playfully at his tie and gave him a gentle nudge.

James took a deep breath, remembering her from university, confident and a little too pushy, although charming company. Leaning against his arm she said, "I'm coming to your part of Scotland in a few weeks, perhaps I could call in and see you?" James felt his stomach do a nervous flip. Ruth had a habit of – attaching herself – and being over friendly to the onlooker. Although charming, he remembered her over attention to him in the past and her ability to cajole you into situations. He wasn't going to worry; he had never encouraged her. "You will be going to the meeting in Edinburgh, won't you, James, about six weeks' time to work on finalising the project; it will all be fun. We'll have time to catch up then, and you can take me to one of your favourite eating places." Grinning, she planted a firm kiss on his cheek.

"Ruth, I'm…" But she had turned away and was talking. Staring at the map in front of him, James found his concentration had gone and a niggle of annoyance settled on him.

'Shoreside Refreshments' had been very comfortable, and Helen and Dougal had been almost reluctant to leave especially after the homemade Scottish patties and sausage rolls, which they had demolished while they watched bare-chested men pull two small fishing boats up the beach and start to unload. As they made to leave, the lady from 'Shoreside Refreshments' came with them carrying a huge woven basket, which reminded Helen of the creels the women carried all those years ago on the shieling. Fascinated, she watched her run lightly down to the boats and offer the fishermen food as they laid fresh fish in the basket. Waving goodbye to Shoreside Refreshments and looking at Dougal walking proudly in all his finery, she could hear him singing and hurried to get nearer to hear the words. It seemed the patties and sausage rolls had brought on a song, the tune was catchy.

Some has meat and canna eat
And some wad eat that want it
But we have meat and we can eat
And say the Lord be thankil

94

Dougal turned to look at Helen. "Course that should be said afore ye eat, it's the well-known 'Selkirk Grace', oh, yes." He was quiet for a while, obviously thinking of dinner. She breathed in the salty air feeling relaxed. He suddenly broke the quiet moment. "Bashed neeps and tatties and good old Scottish beef…well, not old…Ye know what I mean."

Grinning from ear to ear lighting up his nordic features he said, "I'm eating at the Sentinel tonight, aye, I looked in to see what we would be eating and that canny cook had me a bashin the neeps."

Seeing Helen's frown he said, "That's swede and tat…potatoes to you." She didn't appear impressed but knew it would be good anyway. "Ye al no guess what's coming after that." He clasped his hands together in a prayer gesture and looked heavenwards and spoke the words as if they were precious. "Typsy Laird, oh, Typsy Laird." Regaining his composure. "That's Scot's Trifle to you, lass, flavoured with Drambuie."

"I like Drambuie; it's my favourite liqueur."

"Ay and so it should be too; it's got whisky at its base." Helen trotted after him as they crossed over to the beach. The lighthouse was in sight now so Helen knew the Sentinel was not far away.

James stood up, his body was aching from sitting so long in one position; he stretched, the meeting was almost at an end now, and the deep longing to be with Helen enveloped him again. He felt pleased that the whole venture had been approached sensitively and would hopefully please the islanders. The chairman stood up. "Last thing, gentlemen…and ladies." He cleared his throat. "We have to approve the written text for the leaflets that are to be distributed to the locals. They need to be clearly informed on the happenings with the coming observatory." There was audible mumbling among the members. "Also there is a holiday company 'Dark Sky's Holidays' that wish to handle that side of it; we will have to leave that in the hands of the islanders. More important that they have the correct information."

"The information leaflet for the locals is as follows." James sat down sighing. He was tired now and just wanted to get back to Helen, now that all the preliminary work was over. Another member stood up. "The Astronomical Society, we thought 'Written in the Stars' a good heading. It needs your approval.

"An opportunity to marvel at the night sky in a place where there is no light pollution. The observatory will be located on Fay Island, sited at Fables Bowl, a perfect site in the earth's structure. It will take in the wonders of the universe.

You can learn how to see celestial animals in the constellations. The schools will be able to visit, getting children interested in astronomy. Our visitors can hope to see the moon's craters, mountains and lunar seas. Many planets like Mars and perhaps a meteor or two and at certain times the spectacular meteor showers. We also hope to offer things like siting of the Andromeda galaxy and other far off destinations." He paused for a moment laughing good humouredly. "It's busy up there now, even manmade satellites. I guarantee you will see bats." The speaker sat down as an appreciative ripple of claps rang around the room. "I take that as a pass."

James waved saying 'see you all in Edinburgh' and made a quick exit. He was humming to himself, looking forward to Helen, dinner and the cosy Sentinel. The barman had told him that it was party night and there would be music, most of the locals could play a musical instrument, and he was really looking forward to this.

Helen slipped her shoes off and felt the cold sand under her toes. Dougal took her shoes from her so she took the liberty of slipping her camera around his neck. Climbing some low rocks and walking along until the sea gurgled in and out of the gaps, she sat down. Looking into the clear water and letting her toes rest on the surface sent an involuntary shudder through her. Dougal cringed. "Ye canna see um, lass, but the crabbies can see your toes." Helen never had been able to resist water. It looked so inviting, but it was icy. "No, no lass," he warned as if he had read her mind. She blew him a kiss thinking to herself he was a real sweetie. Almost closing her eyes the horizon looked two colours of blue tinged with green, as the hazy edges of the folding waves glittered. Longing to be in James's arms, she missed him. Nimbly returning to the sandy beach, she thought about putting her shoes on.

Dougal was making his way along the beach towards the road. Feeling the firm sand beneath her feet did something to Helen. The surroundings were so beautiful, the lushness of the hills and the sky's thin veil of white lace, fractured here and there that her mother used to call Angel's Wings uplifted her making her feel glad to be alive. Dougal stopped and waited for her. Giving way to elation, she took off dancing along the beach stag jumping with one leg bent under her and the other stretched out behind, her arms flung high. Leaping gracefully into split leaps that seemed to soar and hover in mid-air and spinning with her hair flying, laughing as the sea flashed by and Dougal a blur of colour. Breathless, she came up to him. "You're gonna do ya sell a mischief in a minute, lass." But he had a twinkle of admiration on his face. "And then what'll I tell James." Helen put her shoes on and then linked arms with him.

"Tell him I had a lovely day."

Dougal puffed his chest out proudly. "Ay, lass, that's the Fay's air. Like the whisky water, it's magic."

Chapter 16

Dinner was just how Dougal had described it, utterly scrumptious; she knew she shouldn't have had a second helping of dessert, especially hearing a plump lady at the table after her second helping say – a moment on the lips a lifetime on the hips…

Today, at her request, the chambermaid had taken the dressing gown from the bedroom, although James slept in there last night, and there it was on its hanger behind the bar alongside the clay pipe. The barman saw her looking and winked at her while doing a ghostly movement with his arms. So it was now an exhibition item, she didn't mind, knowing she was going to have to relate the happenings as there was so much genuine interest, and it was a recurring story over the years. James had been approached by one of the locals regarding a talk this evening on the observatory and was now in discussion at the bar.

The lounge was filling up, and she was pleased to see some of the locals had brought their wives or girlfriends, and there was a scattering of children who were being ushered into a long room at the side with plenty to amuse them in there. Helen saw Hamish and Megan with the twins arrive and greeted them warmly. "Megan, those cakes you gave Dougal and I the other day were very tasty." She looked down shyly and rummaged in her bag. Hamish looked at her affectionately and took the bag off her. "I'll hold it while you look," then quietly, "she's made you another cake."

Megan hastily added, "It's only a small Dundee, to take home." Helen took the prettily wrapped cake and hugged Megan almost feeling a tear coming. It smelt wonderful and fresh; Hamish took the cake from her.

"I'll put it behind the bar for you." As he turned to go, Helen saw a slim guitar slung across his back. They sat on one of the large cushiony benches against the wall, and Megan wanted to hear the story of Lilly.

Through the crowd, James was smiling across at her. He was looking more relaxed now. Pushing his way through to her, as always Helen's heart missed a beat, he looked so handsome. James had almost reached her when a local linked arms with him. "Ah, James me lad, ye can tell us all about this place we're a gettin," and steered him away in the direction of the bar counter. He was bidding everyone to sit down quietly and listen.

Suddenly questions started to come, thick and fast, but the man that had waylaid James spoke out. "Hey, hey, now wait a wee while James has something to tell us. Questions after." He slapped him on the back. "Off ye go, lad."

Although James had been taken aback, the content of the information interesting held his audience spellbound. "The domed observatory will be a handsome building and blend in with the lie of the land at Fables Basin. It will be housing the most up to date giant telescopes with powerful lenses able to penetrate deep into the universe. The year 1962 is a very exciting year with the Mercury Atlas 6 Rocket due to take off from Cape Canaveral on 20th February, but I don't think the observatory will be ready by then." This brought a laugh. Some of the children had crept out and were sitting cross-legged and just as enthralled as the grownups.

There was a low buzz of chatter now in the background, as James continued. A tall woman with a small drum under her arm asked, "Will we be able to see Saturn with those rings around it?" James smiled, pleased to see the interest.

"Yes, it will, but Saturn isn't the only one with rings; Jupiter, Neptune and Uranus all have rings; they are not quite so distinctive." One of the children put his hand up to ask a question and James pointed to him.

"Will it be possible to see those lovely coloured lights in the sky that come from Iceland?"

"Oh, yes, that's Northern and Southern lights really spectacular."

"At certain times of the year. I don't want to spoil it for you, but, strangely enough, they are only gusts of solar wind but breath-taking shapes and colours and make such enormous formations. We are hoping to see the Asteroid Belt as well." He looked around, but it seemed they still wanted more. "We will be able to see star clusters close up, constellations, nebulae and galaxies, some with the naked eye." Music could be heard; James took this as a sign to call a halt.

Making his way towards Helen, she knew he was pleased with himself and moved over making room for him. The lounge door opened and an attractive redhead squeezed her way in. A head of red hair swung across him stopping him in his tracks. "James, you left without saying goodbye," and kissed him full on the lips, to his astonishment.

The redhead was attractive, pushing out her curves completely blocking his way forward. Helen watched the girl's tactics. She did seem as if she knew James quite well, and he was having difficulty extricating himself and attracting some attention. Helen plainly heard her say, "Don't forget to meet me in Edinburgh, promised to take me to your favourite eating place. I'm looking forward to it; we can go over old times, James." She looked at him meaningfully.

Momentarily uncomfortable and still not able to extract himself, he looked across at Helen with a helpless expression. Returning the look with a reassuring smile, she got up and made for the room with the children. Although the children were interested in the stars, they really wanted to hear more about the clay pipe and white dog. Helen began to tell them about the happenings on her walk when she was lost. Hesitating, should she tell them about the dressing gown and pipe, not wanting to frighten the children. Unaware she had attracted the grownups from behind her, a few chairs were being discreetly arranged so they could also hear the story.

Scanning the bar, she saw the barman brush his hand down the dressing gown sleeve and give her the thumbs up, so, taking a deep breath, "It was like this…" Skipping around a few of the details, she told the story as – gently truthful – as she could. They didn't seem at all worried about the dressing gown but were wide-eyed and enthusiastic.

"I wondered what the dressing gown was doing hanging behind the bar," one of the boys exclaimed. Jock Hamish called out, "Dougal will have that in a glass case and on show to the holidaymakers – I mean star people; he's gonna have a ball."

His twin brother joined in, "Yeah, he'll tell that story a hundred times and each time it will be different."

The children erupted into laughter. Helen jumped as a woman close behind her said, "My husband said it was McTavish coming back for his pipe, but I didna take much notice at the time." A rosy-cheeked woman touched Helen's arm.

"My mother told me about the white dog; she became lost when a sudden mist filled the glen when she was between farms, this was about thirty years ago. She was terrified because of the bogs and ravines, and where ever the dog appeared she made for and after a while, she found she was below the mist. Mother hoped she would follow her home. Everyone loves Lilly."

Music was coming from the other side of the lounge now loudly and people were in full song, others reaching for an assortment of instruments. James came up behind Helen, not in quite the relaxed mood he had been earlier. There was a distinct red imprint of lips on his cheek and another sideways on his lips reaching up to his nose. Helen laughed up at him. "It's not quite your colour, James." He immediately took a snow-white hankie and tried discreetly to remove the stain. Taking the hankie from him and wiping his cheek Helen said, "I think it's indelible lip liner and going to need soap and water." She worked away at it. He took the hankie looking at the red smears, rolling it up, taking it over to the fire and throwing it firmly into the flames.

Indicating he was going upstairs, he disappeared. Helen went to the bar and ordered a coffee, confiding in the barman there was enough Drambuie in the dessert to last her all night, but it was delicious. He smiled warmly at her; he liked this girl from London with Scottish blood. Handing her the coffee in a wide-rimmed cup and hovering over it with the liqueur bottle he said, "Just a wee nip and winking." She sipped slowly and felt the warm glow down to her toes.

Dougal swept up to her looking smart in his plaids. "You can leave that and dance with me. Can ye no do the Scottish Reel?" Actually, yes she could, way back in her dance exams, she had to be able to perform the Scottish Reel and the Highland Fling. Away they went just as James re-appeared and was holding her own on the makeshift dance floor, joining the others and loving it. Now that it was obvious she knew the dance, there were lots of willing partners until James claimed a dance.

Finishing her coffee sitting tightly next to James, she wondered if he was sad to be leaving tomorrow; she knew that it would have been lovely to have had another few days. Her bag was already packed, but she hoped she would see again the friends she had made on Fay Island.

Every now and then, she looked at the dressing gown hanging at the back of the bar and wondered if the local woman tonight had been right about McTavish coming back for his pipe. The pipe had been in the pocket the other night and it had been – out there – a long time.

She felt James kiss her ear and squeeze her to him. "You enjoyed yourself tonight, twinkle toes."

"Yes, I really did," she said looking at him with shining eyes. "The opportunity to do any dancing is wonderful." Hamish's twins came to say goodnight.

"Are you putting the dressing gown back in your bedroom tonight, Helen?" She gave an exaggerated 'no, no…', which brought a squeal of laughter from them as they ran to the door.

Helen hugged Megan and kissed Hamish as he whispered, "Don't forget the cake behind the bar." James kissed Megan and shook hands with Hamish; Helen felt a tug at her heart and felt honoured to have met this family.

Across the room, Dougal was having a quick shuteye; he had been dancing all night. Standing looking at him, he looked so peaceful; she had enjoyed her time with him. He was managing to sleep through the noise.

They made their way to the bar. Smiling at them, she said, "You had them in the palm of your hands tonight, James."

"Yes, I certainly had their interest. By the way, I've quite a lot of leaflet information about the coming observatory; can I leave it with you?"

"Course ye can, lad, it's gonna be a might big talking point, and ye know who will be leading…" The three of them said in unison 'Dougal' laughing together.

Dougal stirred, sat up, looked around and started singing. "Will ye stop that tickling Jock, oh, will ye stop that tickling Jock." Then he sank back making himself comfortable again and closing his eyes.

The barman looked at Helen and inclined his head towards the dressing gown. 'No, no' then towards the clay pipe 'no, no' then held up the cake. 'Yes, yes'. "Away in the morning, James; it's been good to see you again."

Chapter 17

Helen suddenly felt sad at the thought of going home in the morning. Having developed a great affinity for the Fay Island people and the friends she had made in the short time she had been here, it was going to be a bit of a wrench.

The boat wouldn't be leaving until eleven o'clock, and she had already made up her mind to pay 'Shoreside Refreshments' a visit to take home some of the goodies. As she stared into infinity with her thoughts on mouth-watering food, she became aware of James's arm slipping around her and squeezing her to him. Turning slowly noticing a strange look in his eyes. "Helen, let's go to bed." He was staring at her intently; she realised his meaning. His eyes held such promise, knowing now that tonight possibly would be the night she would give herself to him.

In his room, she couldn't help smiling to herself with the memory of the past couple of nights. He gently took her face in his cupped hands allowing his fingers to slide down onto her cheek then neck. Kissing each breast as he lowered himself onto one knee and looking up at her. "I want to marry you."

Helen waited. "Is that, as in, will you marry me?"

Jumping up and lifting her off her feet, as they both landed on the centre of the bed. His voice came in a rush. "Yes, yes, yes." They were both laughing.

"Will you marry me, my darling? I will love and cherish you all our life." His eyes simmered with passion.

"Yes, my darling James, I've wanted you to ask me for a long time." And now it was happening.

"You know I love you, James, with every part of my body and soul."

They lay quietly enjoying the muffled sounds of the sea. Helen sat up. James was still holding her hand. "It's all right. I'm going to have a bath."

"No, darling, we are going to have a bath." He was still holding her hand. As they stood together, he kissed each one of her fingers, slowly starting to undress her.

Standing motionless, watching the water deepen as the bath bubbles spread and popped, aware of his naked body, a feeling of lightheaded delight surrounded her.

He longed to hold her tightly to him but knew she was wrestling with shyness. Lifting her gently and feeling the touch of her skin against his own, he had the sudden urge to abandon the bath and go straight to bed. Smiling down at her, he was openly enjoying her nakedness. "You are a vision of loveliness," he said kissing her as he lowered her into the water.

Looking at him, unashamedly experiencing a thrill of what the coming night would hold. He looked so strong and handsome that she had to stifle a gasp at his physique as he stepped into the bath. Sitting down, he pulled her slowly towards him. "You know I love you, Helen, and would never do anything to hurt you." Feeling him against her body was a wonderful feeling, something she had been dreaming of. Laying in the warm water with him, scooping water gently across her breasts felt relaxingly heavenly.

With an overwhelming feeling of love, stretching her body against him and excitement rising, she kissed his neck, then his chin and reaching his lips, soft, moist and slightly parted, she felt his quick intake of breath. Between kisses caressing her beautiful body against him, remembering how she danced, he deftly removed the bath plug with his foot.

Laughing as he rolled her over, lifting her slippery body and stepping out of the bath placing her feet on the floor and wrapping her in a bath towel. Looking into the loving smile she had come to know as she snuggled into him. "I'm longing to be your husband." Lifting her chin to look at him, he looked deep into her eyes causing a quiver to ripple along her back. "I won't disappoint you." The look lingered, then, suddenly lifting her to lay over his shoulder, Helen smiled to herself, she felt like an ancient cavewoman, looking down his tanned back and taut pale cheeks.

Lying comfortably between the sheets, she suddenly felt shy as her hand slowly clutched her throat. Watching him rub the droplets from his legs and arms, sighing inwardly at the sight of his powerful body, she suddenly thought of Angus and Mary. Should she wait for her wedding night? Understanding her expression, he slipped in beside her. "Don't worry, my precious darling, we will only go as far as you want."

Turning towards him and clasping the handsome face, between her hands, kissing the man she loved passionately, knowing she was about to enjoy happiness beyond her widest dreams.

In the bar, lots of whispering chatter could be heard. Dougal stood with his elbow on the bar and a large grin on his friendly face. "I tell eey, the lass is no in err room." He was unable to suppress excited laughter. "I tell eey, ers no in er room." He rubbed his hands together in glee. "Oh, they make a great couple."

Chapter 18

The Snow Goose cut a path through the strong current. A sharp breeze was holding Helen's hair flat to the windward side of her head. Half closing her eyes, she could still see coastline of Fay bringing a feeling of regret at leaving.

Several of the islanders had turned up at the quayside to see them off. Hamish and Megan, with the twins giving them a picture they had drawn, not to be looked at until they were home. Dougal had almost shed a tear saying it was the most fun he'd had in a long time, and the owner of 'Shoreside Teas' had given them a large bag of still warm tempting smelling patties, remembering how Helen and Dougal had enjoyed them in her tearooms.

The barman of the Sentinel wanted to know when they would be coming back. Helen had certainly been the source of interest and was well liked.

Feeling a warm glow of contentment, with the sure feeling of her new friends and looking across at James chatting comfortably with a group of men, she hoped fervently she would see them all again.

Now, leaving the Snow Goose with James tucking her arm under his, they could see Angus sitting on a bench outside the shipping hut. A wide smile spread across his face as he saw them, going readily into his outstretched arms for the familiar hug taking her back to her childhood for a fleeting moment.

James began to tell Angus how pleased he was with the progress of the observatory and had brought some copies of the write up they had given to the islanders, knowing he would be interested.

James noticed Helen had dropped back a little and was holding her camera. "I'll tell you more about it on the way home, just waiting for Helen to catch up. What is she doing?"

Clutching her camera and scanning the dispersing passengers, Helen was trying to keep her nerve. As soon as she had heard the voice, she knew where it had come from, wildly taking shots of the people around hoping she would be lucky enough to catch the owner of the 'voice'; she was sure he hadn't been on the boat and was somewhere in the crowd.

Back in the lodge's cosy kitchen, Mary sat wide-eyed, listening to Helen excitedly relate the happenings of the last few days. When she reached the part of the – moving – dressing gown and the white dog, Mary slowly made the sign of the cross against herself, 'Jesus Joseph Mary'. Helen smiled; she knew Mary had enjoyed hearing about the people that were now her friends and the happenings. "Mary, you would have liked the people of Fay Island, perhaps we will all go back there one day."

"That's strange, lass; I'm sure that was a name Matty mentioned, McTavish, she was often back and forwards to one or another of the islands and that was a friend she made. I think somewhere there is a photo. Och, I'll come across it." Helen put her arm around Mary.

"James has got something to tell you."

Angus came in with a big bottle of wine and some scotch whisky. James followed with a tray of glasses. "We've got something to celebrate, Mary, tell her, lad." James came over to Mary and kissed her on the side of her cheek speaking softly into her ear as she felt about in her pocket for her hankie. Angus put a drink into her hand as she silently started to cry.

Handing a glass to Helen he said, "You have a fine lad there; I know you will be very happy." Helen went and knelt down alongside Mary.

"Please don't cry."

"Och, I'm no crying," she said dabbing her eyes and pressing her hankie into her pocket. "Let's drink to a new era in the glen." Angus had a gleam in his eye. He had hoped right from the start that this would eventually be the outcome and he was very pleased with the progress. He put his arm around Mary's shoulder. He knew what her tears were for; she thought she would be losing Helen to the castle, and it had come as a shock.

Suddenly they remembered the Shoreside Refreshment's tasty patties and sharing them around, they went well with the wine and whisky. Helen was pleased that Mary was impressed.

The men were talking and James asked for a favour, could they all go to the castle now, together, and tell them the good news. He took Helen's hand. "I love her, and I don't want to wait too long, and I know when we are all together arrangements will start to come together." Lifting Helen's hand and kissing her wedding finger, he said, "I hope you don't mind me being so forward, my darling."

Mary suddenly sprang into life. "Let's be away then, oh, Helen, I'll get your post, and Angus McGregor, you're no goin out in the britches, especially to the castle."

Leaving the company to have a quick freshen up and change into a soft white voile top with delicate lace at the scoop neck line, Helen brushed her hair and dabbed some perfume by her ears and wrists.

Looking at her reflection, James would be happy. They both looked as though Fay Island had done them good. Skipping down the stairs and remembering to collect the last five patties for Molly, Katriana, Ginty, Andrew and Stuart. Breathing in the aroma and wishing she had bought more as well as the gift.

Watching Helen, he didn't have to ask if she had enjoyed Fay Island. Looking at her relaxed manner, Angus knew.

Happily chatting on the way to the castle, Mary was full of questions. Pulling up as near the door as she could and watching them tumble excitedly out, feeling a wave of happiness, she caught sight of Andrew with the baby in his arms; he looked a picture of happiness.

Remembering the bag of patties, she went back to the car to get them. Locking the car knew Stuart was standing close beside her. "Hallo, where did you spring from?" she said giving him a quick smile and walking towards the door.

"Helen, come with me." As she hesitated, he took her arm. He was smiling broadly. "I have something to show you." He squeezed her arm. "It's a surprise."

Letting her arm go and extending his hand, come on indicating towards the stables and dimness of the bullpens. Helen didn't take up the offer of his hand but followed him. "Stuart, James will be wondering where I am." He cast her a sideways glance with the hint of a twinkle in his eye. Looking so like his brother, there was now a boyish grin, and he was pointing in the pen. "Look, our new arrival."

Immediately melting, as the newborn calf looked at her, blinking, then shook its head making its ears look big. "Oh she's…he's…lovely". Slowly turning her towards him, he kissed her lovingly.

"Just like you."

Turning away from him she asked, "What did you do that for?"

"Because I've missed you."

Stammering a little, she said, "…Well don't…do it again." Stepping back and looking at him, she softened. "Stuart, you and I are going to be brother and sister in law." And she waited for his reaction. He was staring at her, unblinking. "James asked me to marry him, and I said yes."

Slowly his face changed as he took in the news, allowing the grin to return. "Well, that's different." Putting a friendly arm around her shoulders and planting a quick kiss on her cheek, he added, "I'm allowed a brotherly kiss – I hope."

They walked amicably towards the door just as James was coming out of the door, a frown furrowing his brow as he looked at them. Stuart put out his hand to shake his brother's, and in his usual good-natured way said, "First to hear your wonderful news, you lucky boy." Pointing to himself, then to Helen, he said, "First to see the new arrival." James was taken aback.

"New arrival…" The brothers walked quickly to the bullpens talking excitedly. Helen felt a wave of relief settle over her as she entered the castle.

The patties were received with great relish and Katriana was pleased with her son's news. "It will be good for the family and another wedding is so exciting; it will be like Andrew and Ginty all over again." James was pleased to see his mother smiling, but in his heart, he knew it would be a little different to his cousin's; he was already making plans in his head.

Overwhelmed with all the hugs and kisses of congratulation and really surprised how much the new baby had grown, his hair now brushed to one side and a subtle auburn. Light blue eyes looked at her from a contented face. Ginty told her his eyes would probably change colour in the next few weeks, but she hoped not.

Molly, Mary and Katriana were deep in conversation and the intense excitement could be felt all around the room. Ginty and Helen sat together while Andrew and Angus put the baby to bed. James and Stuart came in all smiles praising the new calf and opening some bottles to celebrate, and drinks were handed around.

James held his glass up. "I'm the happiest man alive," and sipped his drink, the company followed. "We haven't set a date yet and I haven't even bought my Helen a ring, but I know before today is over there will be a few things arranged." He went and stood by Helen's side. "This will be a wedding to remember, my darling." He flung his arms wide. "Everyone is invited." Laughing up at him, she drank her wine and thought about her friends on Fay Island and all her dance friends in London.

Suddenly, she remembered the post Mary had given her. Settling herself in one of the cosy armchairs as the chatter went on around her and looking through the envelopes recognising immediately her brother's handwriting, reading and squealing with delight she said, "James, my brothers and their wives are paying us a visit; they want to see the Highland Games in seven weeks' time." Mary clasped her hands together.

"Oh, how lovely. Isn't that just the best news." Angus smiled to himself; he thought there had been some other news to top that.

"Well…now we know the date of the wedding, lass." A burst of laughter filled the room.

"They say they want to stay and are giving us plenty of notice."

Looking across at James, he smiled at her then looked heavenwards. "I love your brothers. Wonderful, seven…long weeks it is then." Andrew slapped him on the back and was laughing with Stuart.

"Being a woman, she's gonna need more like seventeen weeks." Then Stuart caught the look on James's face and shrugged.

Chapter 19

Time seemed to be passing quickly, but Helen, with lots of help, had made quite a few arrangements and now there was only a few ends to pull together. David and Lucinder Balantine had been like two unstoppable forces, full of wonderful ideas, including the throwing open of the Big House with the actual marriage there, but the family chapel was small.

Helen had opted for two huge marquees to be erected in the grounds of the Big House with connecting walkways through and an orchestra in one and a band in the other. Then later on in the evening, they planned to move into the large ballroom but only the ballroom thinking of David and Lucinder's beautiful plush carpeting and delicate decor. Also the possibility of the ceremony taking part on the long terrace above the steps.

There was a vast amount of staff arranged and the catering, flowers and the many lights that were appearing was becoming exciting. Katriana would have liked James married in the castle chapel, which gave Helen a slight problem. Stuart came to her rescue voicing his opinion. "Mother, as lovely as it would be, there is no way we could accommodate the number of people that are coming to see your eldest son married. Helen has the right idea, keep them in one place."

Since James had been preoccupied recently, Helen had been grateful for Stuart and Angus's help and advice. Something Stuart was now dealing with was the possible amount of people who would be coming on horseback and carriages. Dear Angus admitting he was well out of his depth with something this big was in discussion with David Balantine about the cars and Helen's dance friends.

Today, they were going on a wedding dress trip. Although she knew she could have had a dressmaker come to the lodge, this was much more fun.

Helen had hired a 10-seater mini bus and Molly, Mary, Ginty, Katriana and now Lucinder with Helen were on their way. Leaning back, enjoying the fact that they now had a driver, Helen's new chauffeur. Mary also had her own staff now, which she had complained about but was getting used to having more time.

Angus was only too happy to have two gardeners but not to touch his precious rose garden.

Lunch had been a happy conversation time. The ten-seater was hardly big enough for all the parcels and caused lots of laughs on the way home.

The workmen erecting the two marquees had told Lucinder and David that they had come from part of an order for the Highland Games and that they would have to get them to the site as soon as possible the morning after the wedding, just leaving three days to the opening of the games, but they had been grateful as marquees of this size were very few.

Angus had told James that David Balantine wanted to speak with him, so it was while the women were wedding dress shopping the men took the opportunity in the late afternoon to have a meeting at the castle. The subject of rustling was getting worrying and nearer home. Over the last two months, David had two cows in calf to champion stud bulls, stolen. "They were over with my top stockman. Electrified gate and fence, don't know how they did it."

The outcome of the meeting was that they would ride out one day and see if they could find out where this gang of thieves were hiding out and how they were operating. "The lands are vast; we ride the boundaries almost every day."

"We've all got a lot to lose so we've got to do something though, James." David's voice was troubled. "We will get together and decide on a date; I suggest we tell no one about our plans; I'll take my top stockman."

"We'll take two of our head cattle men, all right with you, James?" And we will get this done as soon as possible.

The next morning, Helen and James made an early start. Choosing a ring was easy; they were all beautiful. The roast at lunch was tasty. Helen was anxious to collect the photos she had put in first thing this morning, and after the wedding dress trip, she had seen enough of shops for a while so they made for home.

On the way home, she studied the photos living again the happy time on Fay Island knowing she had been right to buy all coloured rolls of film. The ones of the sheep and cattle with the orange sinking sun colouring their backs were good. The one of the bull deep in the contours of the valley were quite faint, and she would look at them later with a magnifying glass. As she had been prepared for, there were no images of the dog Lilly.

The air was electric today at the lodge; Helen's dance friends were arriving for the hen and stag party, including two of the male dancers.

Mary had prepared the lounge and dining room, as they were going to stay at the lodge first then into town. The caterer's van had just delivered the food for the evening. Mary had found it hard not to be doing the cooking for the company, but she was getting used to it and revelling in being able to be one of the guests.

It was a wonderful feeling being surrounded by her friends, colourful, happy and with a zest for life. All talking at once, they made a great fuss of Mary and Angus. Claudette grinned at Angus. "So you're the one who grows lovely roses." But before he could reply, Jo Jo came over.

"Ah, yes, roses, but I like the bit about your strawberries." And gently he pinched the side of his face.

Mary and Angus had felt a bit flustered with all these people that seemed as if they had just arrived from another planet. But after an hour, they had grown used to them and were thoroughly enjoying the friendly noisy bunch.

When Mary was helping Angus on with his coat, he was almost wishing he was staying with these people or rather they could all meet up. They were certainly enjoyable company, but he dutifully prepared to leave as the members of the stag party arrived to collect him. The girls shut Helen in the kitchen telling her it was bad luck to see the groom the night before your wedding, then went to give the Scotsman the once over.

There was soon lots of laughing as the two parties met and gelled. Stuart lost no time in acquainting himself with the dancers. It was another hour before the stag party left, waiting for the other two men and seeing Helen rescued from the kitchen.

The two male dancers dragged themselves away from the interesting Katriana finally and asked Mary where they could put their sleeping rolls. Mary was a little confused by this. She had wondered what was in the large rolls they had arrived with. Helen explained all nine would be sleeping at the lodge, no question of splitting them up, and they all divided themselves between the three bedrooms upstairs and Claudette and Helen had Mary and Angus's spare twin-bedded room downstairs.

The cars arrived to take them to town, and they streamed out of the lodge singing 'Let's Paint the Town Red Let the Fun Begin'. A worried Mary hurried up to Helen. "Helen, quick…"

"Mary, what's the matter?" she asked looking at her worried expression.

"We seem to…er…have acquired…some more – bodies, who are they?" The girls laughed at the two male dancers now wearing tartan caps and ginger wigs.

"We've never seen them before in our lives; they're not one of us, Mary, throw them out." They laughed as a couple of the girls pushed them into the garden just as David and Lucinder arrived. The male dancers tipped their caps to them.

"Good evening," then turning back called out, "we've been thrown out of better places than this," and went into the arm on the shoulder routine singing…

"Underneath the arches, I dreamed my dreams away." Their voices were rich and the others joined in and David and Lucinder, being American, thought it quite natural as Mary was attempting an explanation.

Chapter 20

Curled up in her armchair, the lodge was quiet. Looking through the photos of Fay Island, she had that warm special feeling. Now, standing at the open window looking out across the vista, she knew that summer was advancing. The land was aglow with buttercups and gowan, vetch and harebell, the little Scottish blue bell. Breathing in the morning scent, she stood like a statue.

Just a mild headache crossed her brow, but all was right with the world. In the distance, the loch shone, a little sparkle here and there as the sun slipped out from behind a cloud. Surveying the contours, knowing the river would be tumbling through the tree-lined gorge and salmon would be leaping upstream. How she loved this land feeling an air of magic and excitement of mixed feeling as the view would be slightly different tomorrow.

Looking down at the circle of white flowers that formed her headdress, she thought of her mother and father and Aunt Matty. Her day would have been complete if they'd been here to share it with her. Looking into the far distant green fells and wooded slopes, she felt a hypnotic pull. The whole vista with its intensifying beauty filled her with love.

A knock on her bedroom door and Mary floated in, her lilac outfit was just perfect for her, and Helen could see she felt good. "I found some more hairgrips for your headdress; we don't want that sailing away on the wind. Do you want me to help you with it?" Standing back and looking at her, she said, "Oh, Helen, you look beautiful. James won't be able to believe his eyes." Turning to the mirror, she sat down allowing Mary to fuss over her. "I'll just close the window, lass."

1U With her headdress secured under her three quarter veil, the two of them came halfway downstairs. "Now, you wait there a wee moment." Mary finished going down the stairs and picking up her hat off the table, placed it on her head, calling Angus. As he came through the door, she put Helen's camera in his hand, gently pushing him forward. "Doesn't she look lovely?" Angus stared unblinking. "Well, come on then, take the wee girl's photo." Picking up her box of confetti, she said, "See you in church, Helen." Then she stopped, putting her hand to her mouth. "I mean on the terrace, see that you're not late, Angus." Then she glided out into the sunshine.

In the doorway, they stood under the arch of roses enjoying the perfume. Angus breathed it in. "Matty's favourite. Do you think she's here?" He held his arm for her.

"Och, I think they're all here, they're no gonna miss a weddin."

They walked together to the waiting car; it was decked with white satin ribbons, fluttering in the breeze. Mary, the two bridesmaids and pageboy drove off waving. Helping to arrange her dress, he slipped in beside her. "This is a very proud day for me, Helen and for your mum and dad." He nodded to the driver. They drove slowly down the drive, both enjoying the peacefulness of the moment. Lifting her bouquet, she smelt the delicate roses, then slipped her ring onto the other hand.

The sight that met them took their breath away, a sea of happy people, colour and music, a moving kaleidoscope, she was able to see James's farmer friends and folk from the many farmsteads; there seemed to be hundreds of people. Looking around at the array of large hats and different outfits gave her the feeling it was one large garden party and some Fay people. The feeling was wonderful. The view looked unreal ablaze with light. Music could be heard mixed with happy chatter. The large carved urns were spilling over with flowers. A pale pink carpet covered the whole terrace and the man that was to perform the ceremony stood like a statue in his gold and white robe. Angus smiled proudly.

The sight of James, as always, made her catch her breath, and as he saw her leave the car, he put both hands to his lips blowing her hands full of kisses. The same weakness came over her as she looked at the strong handsome man so confident, that she was about to marry. Her happiness was overflowing.

Stuart by his side almost looked like twins, although Stuart was not quite as tall as James. His mother Katriana looked slim and elegant in pale apple green and cream and Andrew's wife Ginty was colourful in a flower design material. The three men standing together in their kilts and full regalia, proudly wearing their family tartan. Mary was in dove grey silk and Molly cerise. The dancers were in an array of London fashion, adding a big splash of colour to the already heady scene. Helen smiled to herself having a good idea where they had come from, as dancers were always hard up. She intended to change this situation.

Helen and Angus drank in the scene. "Och, you remember this for the rest of your life, lass." They walked towards the steps as the two bridesmaids and pageboy ran up the steps. Molly tactfully collected them and brought them down again as they were to walk behind Helen and Angus up the steps.

The procession mounted the steps. On the terrace, Angus put Helen's hand into James's whispering, "Take good care of her, lad," then joined the other kilted family members, swelling the picture.

They framed a backdrop of family and friends, making an elegant picture. David, Angus, James, Stuart and Andrew, dressed in their family tartans and in full regalia, made a breath-taking sight. Katriana, Ginty, Molly and Mary provided the elegance alongside them and cameras clicked nonstop.

James held Helen's hand unable to speak. His eyes spoke of his love for her. The Reverend McAllan in his gold and white stepped forward. The ceremony began.

Wedding celebrations were in full swing and friendships made and enjoyed. Helen was trying to get around to all her guests, but there were so many and so much to say. Pleased to see many of the friends she had made on Fay Island here with her and James. Dougal was in fine form, no sign of the golf outfits. Hamish, Megan and the twins, the lady from Shoreside Refreshments and the dancers. Helen couldn't have asked for more.

As dusk fell, throngs of people moved into the ballroom as it became a sea of light from the many chandeliers. There were gasps of surprise and appreciation at the luxurious surroundings. It was so good to see so many people really enjoying themselves and each other. Helen knew she was glowing, watching her brothers let their hair down. James was dancing with Lucinda and David with Ginty. Helen remembered the last time she was here, and Stuart was missing then; she smiled to herself; Stuart was missing now, hoping he was behaving himself. He was a very attractive man.

Dancing couples were floating about the ballroom in wonderful dresses. There was going to be a highland dance where the ladies wore kilts, which was just about to start, the pleats flicked attractively about their legs.

Helen noticed her dance friends collecting in a corner at one end of the ballroom. There were flashes of sequins and she was filled with a warm feeling as she guessed they were going to perform. Hurrying to find James, they sat together and enjoyed the clever routine, earning lots of clapping. Still lots of cameras clicked, and Dougal suggested they come to Fay Island.

Stuart was now in his element taking it upon himself to look after the dancers collecting a few addresses on the way…

A few guests were leaving, and it was getting close to the time Helen and James would leave for the night. Not knowing, as James maintained it was a surprise. Later, on the steps the congregation saw them off to a noisy goodbye but laughing because they would be back for breakfast.

Driving into the hills and heading for shieling country, Helen was a little puzzled. Looking at her husband hardly able to believe they were married once again filled with happiness. What on earth was the surprise? It was dark now and they had stopped. "Just a little walk, Helen." A little way ahead, she could see a shaft of light. They walked a little further, now Helen was beginning to get worried. Knowing they were deep in shieling country.

Able to make out the outline of a cleit, she suddenly realised why they were here. This was the surprise. Feeling a mixture of love and apprehension, she looked up at him.

Way below them, lights sparkled through the black pines from a tiny church. Faintly on the wind, a Gaelic choir were singing.

Lifting her into his arms and lowering his head, he entered the cleit. Now he was able to stand upright, he turned slowly in a circle anxious for her to see the extent of his labours over the last few weeks. "You do like it?" Her face was a picture.

"So this is what you've been getting up to." Pulling his head closer and kissing his questioning mouth, she said, "I adore it, husband of mine." Studying her, he replied, "Yes, I am," looking at her with a proud love that he was struggling to control at the moment.

Sitting her on the edge of the velvet covered bed, he knelt between her knees and cuddled her to him. "No shyness tonight, Mrs Helen McKlinross." Knowing how tired they both were, she started to remove his top garment.

"Not shy…just a little…apprehensive. I need to know that I…please you." He had been removing her clothing and now from a tissue parcel slipped a beautiful negligee on her.

"I'll let you know in the morning." His eyes registering slight amusement.

They looked into each other's eyes; there was that strange light she had seen there before. Laying side by side, James raised himself slightly and leaned over her. "…James…I've never…"

"Shh, my darling, it will be all right, close your eyes." Relaxing and enjoying the feel of velvet on her near nakedness and the touch of his skin, she listened to the deep emotion in his voice.

"We are swimming in the pool by the waterfall, and I am Ross and you are my Kerry; I love you, my precious darling." His love was gentle and considerate, making the most of every second. He almost took her on Fay Island but knew there would be a better time and place with future memories to enjoy and not forgoing the trust of Angus and Mary.

Stretching luxuriously and blinking through the dimness of the cleit into speckled sunlight shimmering through the trees, Helen was aware of the heady aroma of the cleit and James standing by the opening. The sunlight behind him showing all his manly physique and handsomeness, remembering last night she felt happiness and a great contentment, knowing their life together would be something to look forward to in the years to come.

Throwing himself down beside her making her squeal, he put a brown paper parcel in her hands. "Sorry, I meant to give you this last night…"

Wide eyed, she said, "…I haven't bought you anything – oh, James." He smiled into her eyes.

"I haven't bought you anything, except that negligee you're almost wearing." Watching her open the parcel, he felt excitement rising. Helen thought she was going to cry; there on her lap were her beloved sandals that Aunt Matty had bought her. Slipping them on, she walked around the cleit not believing she had them once again.

"It's the best present you could have given me." Coming into his arms, she felt the excitement too.

"You gave me yourself, and that's all I wanted, you're my Kerry, my wife and the love of my life, and I want to make love to you forever." Laying back down.

Exhausted and happy, they drove back to the Big House 'Mount Eagle Place'. The caterers were serving the many tables in the sunken garden; smell of breakfast told the couple they were hungry. They laughed, weathered the jokes and ate heartily. Helen's family and all the dancer friends had been invited out by the men, and they were being taken to see the red deer then on to some famous gardens. Too soon, it was all over and the dancers were on their way back to London, being together had done them all good. Helen's family had really enjoyed, promising to visit soon.

Remembering the Tossing of the Caber among other strong-armed games, Helen was taken by the sheer strength of these men. It looked like a giant telegraph pole; they had to get it tossed over the top. An upright pole supported from the waist, their grip looked unsure, then they would heave it over. Helen would hold her breath as sometimes the pole would fall the wrong way, bringing a gasp from the crowd.

There was a re-enactment of the attack by the MacDonalds and the Campbells, which looked very real to Helen and reminded her of some of the paintings she had seen. It brought shouts from the men. Later the marching bands were colourful in their tartan kilts, their sporrans rolling across their knees from side to side as they walked. Just one thing clouded the day and made Helen feel a slight annoyance. Redhead Ruth surfaced. The men were standing at the bar in the drinks tent; James was talking and was turned away from her when she suddenly playfully jumped on his back, drawing a few puzzled looks from Helen's family.

Now she had acquired herself an invite to the castle. Thinking ahead, Helen would see if Stuart would help her out and keep the redhead entertained. It seemed to work like a dream until James had to drive her to the town instead of Stuart.

Helping Ginty to put the children to bed was easy tonight as they were almost asleep on their feet, but it gave Helen the chance to tell her all about Fay Island and what had happened over there. "I'm so looking forward to you living here in the castle, Helen." Confiding in her now about being certain the voice she heard when they left the Snow Goose was one of the men who stole Out of the Blue and was responsible for her blow on the head. Ginty was puzzled. "You must tell James, Helen."

"When I have the photos, I have a strong feeling it is him deep in the dell."

Chapter 21

During the next few years, workmen made a few changes to the interior of the castle. The east and west turrets now housed lifts, something new, enabling easy access to three upper floors and creating great excitement. The top floor of the east turret was now Katriana's private space; she had moved large boxes of photos and keepsakes. A full-length mirror positioned to reflect the view from the window. A plum coloured velvet suite with gold tassels and fringe and her favourite French chaise longue. Most important for both was the large long range telescope giving extensive views to the horizon.

It had taken quite a few months, but eventually, Katriana had acquired planning permission to create a proper window. The two long narrow slits that were the original gaps to fire arrows through, now joined up to make a proper window, giving breath-taking views to the horizon.

Helen had turned her turret room into a place to sketch, paint and cover the walls with pictures and photos. A comfortable bed sofa and a cane rocking chair. The telescope fascinated her and could become her time waster making her late down for dinner at times, but James loved her space; it was comfortable and she was delighted with it. When he had time, he would often stretch out on her bed sofa and watch her sketch.

This year Katriana had commissioned a portrait of James and it now hung on the wall partway up the second staircase. Every time Helen passed, it made her smile looking at him smiling back, his handsome features captured perfectly by the artist. At the top of the stairs was the portrait of his father. This painting intrigued her; she would have liked to know this man. Studying it, she could feel the difficulty the man was experiencing to keep still long enough for the artist to catch the likeness of this vibrant man. Her eyes could see a zest for life. This man had been happy. His intelligent eyes seemed to twinkle as she studied his face; they danced a message of warmth and romance.

Looking back at James's portrait, she had the same feeling. The startling likeness to his father, the unmistakeable lift to the corner of his mouth, a characteristic she had come to know well.

At the top of the staircase, Helen felt she wanted to sit down, so perched carefully on the top stair, feeling the nausea coming on again but smiling to herself. Tomorrow she would go to see the doctor hoping fervently he would be able to confirm that she was pregnant. After all this time and now, perhaps it had finally happened.

Feeling a sudden rush of excitement as she did a calculation on her fingers, if she was right and she was pregnant, it would be a spring baby. Standing up smiling, it was her secret at the moment, but all being well she would soon be able to tell her darling James, trying to imagine his face and the rest of the household.

Looking back along the floor-length pictures, Katriana had told her this morning that she had managed to persuade Stuart to sit for his awaited portrait, something he had been sidestepping for a long time. Helen knew he would be just like his father and find it difficult to sit still for long, but it would be something to look forward to; they were a handsome family and it would grace the staircase.

Deciding to get washed and changed, she would go to the lodge and meet the Balentines. They had taken great care of Mount Eagle Place, but there had been a whisper that they would be returning to America. Thinking about the fabulous paintings and artwork, all the statues in the upper hallways, like the armour and weapons, Helen hadn't seen inside the Big House to know what was there before. Those beautiful carpets that made everywhere look colourfully expensive. The statues in the grounds and extensive lighting. For now, she was at a loss on how it would be worked out, but it wouldn't be a problem.

As always, Mary and Angus were pleased to see her, enjoying the warm hugs she always held her arms out for, knowing Mary would start bustling about and Angus stop what he was doing and give her all his attention. "Mary, hope it's all right, Lucinda and David calling in for a cup of tea." Helen waited for what she knew would happen next.

"Angus, get those trousers off. I'm no having you see company in those."

The Balentines at the Big House had asked to see Helen at her convenience, which set her wondering. Noticing Lucinder had been limping sometimes and didn't always accompany David. It turned out that the couple were now planning to return to America.

Helen invited them to tea at the lodge and could immediately see that Lucinder was in some discomfort but just as attractive as always. They agreed a date a couple of months ahead. They would be a great loss to Helen and what about Mount Eagle. The great house could not stand empty. David had already offered his stock to the boys, and they had agreed a price and would be settling up at the end of their tenancy. Until then, it would be business as usual and the search for the rustlers carried on. Lucinder asked about all the historic goods in Mount Eagle Place, as they would like to take some of them back to America.

After they had left, Helen decided to ask Mary about Aunt Matty's count; it was the first she had heard about it and was anxious to know more. The solicitor had already told her she had already sold some of her property in Park Lane London. Helen had never known her to have property in Park Lane, although when Helen now and again rode in Rotten Row on her aunt's visits, she had always said she had some business to attend to and then they would go to Lyons Corner House for lunch and listen to the elegant woman playing the harp while they ate.

Angus sighed. "It was a long time ago, lass." He was washing his hands and scrubbing his nails. Helen waited patiently as he settled himself and Mary came in with a tray of tea and oatcakes and scones. "Matty had met the gentleman on a train when she was visiting Italy and he had visited her in her apartment taking her out and visiting some famous gardens."

"Aye, he didna tell her they were his," Mary interrupted.

Angus continued, "He wanted to marry her; they had known each other for quite a while." Mary put her cup down.

"Oh, she was a pretty little thing then. He used to take her to glamorous balls and garden parties, and she dressed beautifully." Angus put his cup down.

"Are ye goin to let me tell the story, woman!" Mary sat back and took a deep breath and had a dreamy look come into her eyes.

"…Not all of it."

Looking from one to the other, Helen was pleased to know Matty had romance in her life and learned that the count was a millionaire, but the war intervened so they decided to marry before he went off to fight. "It was complicated." Angus had a frown creasing his brow. Mary continued, "It was a tragedy; he was found dead in bed with his two faithful dogs alongside him. His butler had said he went to lie down because he wasn't feeling well." Mary was looking into her cup as if she were reading her tealeaves. "They said it was natural causes."

"So that explains the uniform in Matty's cupboard; it's been there years; she used to show it to my brothers, said it belonged to a dear friend of hers."

"Your aunt was heartbroken" – looking at Angus – "we looked after her as best we could, but we didn't seem to be much help, poor lass." Angus shrugged his shoulders. "He left her everything he had."

Mary's excited voice broke in, "That's why she was advised to invest the bulk of the money in property, that's how she came to own those in Park Lane. Angus, we'll have to find the photos for Helen, not that I like going through Matty's things."

As Helen pondered the newest revelations of her aunt, it began to make sense where most of the wealth had come from. Helen had loved her aunt, generous and kind she had paid for all their schooling and seen her through dance training. The family had always enjoyed an extremely comfortable home. Starting to think she had better make tracks for the castle and aware of a twinkling of an idea starting in her head, she kissed them both goodbye for now. She pulled away from the lodge and looked across at the Big House already seeing an emerging School of Dance, all types of dance, possibly an education quarter. Her mind was spinning with ideas; she would talk it over with Katriana and see what she thought, wondering how much more there was to learn about her aunt.

Walking along the lake edge hand in hand, James and Helen were enjoying the news today that Helen was indeed carrying James's baby. He was bursting with pride and could hardly contain himself. The breeze now lifting her hair, he felt a great love for the girl he had met by the burn.

A silent hunting harrier lifted from the long grass; it rose with exquisite fluidity. They both watched, its undersides pristine, speckled and white plumage almost gleaming in the sunlight. Its shadow skimmed across them as it went soaring into the distance. Just for a moment, the hills behind it were aglow.

The sky was changing, clouds skimming fast being reflected in the lake. James put his arm around her shoulders, time to go in. "Let's go and tell the family." Lots of congratulations were in order. Although Ginty said nothing, she had an idea something was going on a couple of weeks ago. Molly was the same, but this was exciting times, another baby in the castle; it couldn't come quick enough for them all.

Lewis, Helen's chauffeur had always treated her carefully; having a great liking for Helen, now treated her like a delicate piece of expensive china and wouldn't let her carry anything. Helen was flattered at first but found gradually it became tiresome.

Everyone seemed to be knitting and there were balls of wool everywhere. Andrew had sat on one at breakfast and Stuart was dragging one along caught in his shoe. It had brought a lot of fun, and Katriana was embarking on the mammoth task, to crotchet a pure white shawl just like she did for Andrew and Ginty.

Helen found she was always tired and the baby was growing fast; the doctor had told her several times it was quite a big baby. Thinking that big, might mean long, as at times Helen thought there wasn't going to be much more room and the baby was becoming very active especially at night, adding to her tiredness.

Chapter 22

Sitting in the comfortable armchair near the long windows, Helen could see far into the clear vista. The sky was dotted with grey and white clouds against the palest blue. In the far distance, the horizon looked a pearl colour. Knowing the castle was a long way off in that direction and she wondered how they were all getting on.

The doctor had suggested she spend her last two to three weeks at the lodge so as to be nearer for him or the hospital. Dearest James came in at some time everyday, but he was looking tired. The rustling problem was becoming serious and the farmers and landowners for hundreds of miles around were now pressing for a get together to try to solve the problem as the police didn't seem to be getting very far. Even with the photos, which they were now sure was the champion bull Out of the Blue hadn't seemed to have helped much.

Mary came in with a tray for elevenses and settled herself in a nearby chair, pulling another nearer. Angus will be in shortly. Mary handed the cups around them smiling broadly. "You know, your mother sat in that very same armchair when we were all waiting for you."

"Tell me about it, Mary."

"Well, now, I havter say, lass, it seemed you couldna make up your mind, one minute you were coming, the next you changed your mind. Your poor mother. The doctor came twice, but it was false alarms, the poor wee man he was no happy. He took your mother into hospital in the end." Mary took her cup and fluffed up the cushions. Leaning back, she looked at Helen. "Funny, your mum said you would probably be a dancer." She replaced the cushion as Helen touched her arm. "You were a lively little bairn, always tap dancing against her ribs."
in

"So…When did I decide to get born, Mary?" Helen was smiling to herself knowing Mary was enjoying relating the story. A polite cough from Angus as he waved and left the room. "We thought there were about five more days to go, but that canny doctor made her go in there and then. When she was settled, we all came home. Your brothers and Angus and your dad had the train set out and it was going around the table…mm, there were four bairns playing with it." Mary became thoughtful, her brow furrowed. "I was just finishing my woman's magazine, when that new contraption we had started ringing its bell, making me jump up and drop my book. I didna like that telephone wind up thing." She gave an amused look. "It made the boys laugh."

Helen waited a while. "Who was it then?" Mary had been reliving the night twenty-five years ago.

"Och, it was the midwife at the hospital to tell us she had just delivered you." Looking at Helen and shaking her head, she said. "You waited for us to go and the doctor had gone home and then you decided to come, two hours and no problems. Your dear mother was so happy to have a girl bairn. We all hurried back to the hospital. When we passed the nursery with all those wee cots, some pink blankets and some blue, but only one with its feet going."

"I thought I was born at the lodge." Mary held her head up.

"Well, you were…almost." Angus came in with a pale yellow china vase and a hand full of flowers. "Will ye go and get me the glass vase, Angus?" Without moving, he looked at the vase.

"This is quite nice," he said and put the flowers in and held it up for approval. She turned her head towards Helen and hid a smile.

"Angus MacGregor, do you want to sleep in the cupboard tonight?" With a surprised 'not again' making them all laugh.

"I quite like the vase, Mary, thank you, Angus."

Not for the first time, Helen thought how well suited they were, experiencing movement in her womb and a wave of excitement.

By the end of the fourth week, Helen was getting tired, uncomfortable and wishing things would start happening. Seeing James was good medicine. As he clasped her in his arms, she knew he was tired. There were dark rings under his eyes, and she knew he was worrying about many things. Her heart was bursting with love for him as she kissed every part of his face. "It was worth coming all this way for that." He was on his knees and kissed her passionately on her lips and into her neck, then passing his hand gently over her tummy. "How's James Junior today?"

At her anti natal visit, she was relieved to learn the doctor had decided to admit her in to be started, telling her it was quite a big baby. As she had been keeping her hospital bag in her car, her chauffeur drove her straight to the hospital.

Twenty-four hours later, with Mary and Molly on either side of her and James pacing in the waiting room until he couldn't stand hearing Helen's struggle any longer, came in. A little later, the three of them saw the eight pound James Junior present himself to the world with immediate proof of a wonderful pair of lungs.

Mary dabbed her forehead with a hospital tissue. "My…that was hard work, I'm exhausted." Molly guided her friend out of the delivery room and both towards a cup of tea, leaving the young couple alone. "Molly, I know you've had bairns, no wonder they call it labour." She looked down at her hands and arms still able to see the pressure marks.

James's face was a picture, watching the nurse wrap the baby in a blue blanket and lay him in Helen's arms. Kneeling by the bed and leaning towards his wife, he untucked the tiny hand as it immediately held his finger. "Helen, he's beautiful." A few minutes later, he was lifting the baby into his arms. "Come to Daddy."

The next few days gave Helen the chance to talk to the other new mothers now she was back in the ward. In the next bed was Bryony, quiet with dark hair and a new daughter. In conversation, Helen discovered her husband left her when she was five months pregnant. He didn't want children and within three weeks of moving out had moved in with someone else. But Helen was able to talk to her on a brighter topic as Bryony had studied ballet, tap dancing and acrobatics. This subject filled their time. Bryony loved hearing about the London dance school Helen used to belong to. They exchanged addresses and were determined to keep in touch. Helen had given her the lodge address feeling the castle was a little too grand for now.

Taking the opportunity to hold the little five-pound girl, Helen told her she would like a daughter one day. Looking down at her hands, Bryony told her she would make this one do. Noticing the thin covering on the baby's head of ash blond hair against milky white skin, she couldn't help feeling sorry for the disinterested father and what he was missing.

Bryony looked over Helen's shoulder. "I think you've got a visitor." Stuart made his way towards them. "Hallo, girls," he said, treating them both to his attractive smile and kissing them both. "What's this then?" he said taking the baby from Helen and looking at her. "Blond hair, pink blanket." Helen and Bryony laughed as Bryony took her daughter from Stuart.

"Thank you, she's mine." Helen and Stuart walked to the nursery. He picked up the baby Helen pointed out.

"That's more like it." He stroked the dark hair.

"It's nice of you to come, Stuart, everything all right at home?"

"It will be when you're back." Helen gave him a frown. "No, really the children ask every day, is it today Auntie Helen comes home; you seem to have been away ages."

"Oh, Stuart, it seems like ages."

His eyes smiling at her, he said, "We've all missed you."

Walking back to the ward, Helen told him she had to go to sister's office for a few minutes and to take a seat. When she finally returned, she found him sitting comfortably in a chair next to Bryony, chatting happily. Now that Bryony was smiling, Helen noticed how pretty she was with her dark hair framing her face. Her brother-in-law had worked his charm once again; it was good because she hadn't had any visitors, only the first day.

When Stuart was ready to go, he said he would come again and what would they like him to bring them. Straight away, Bryony said, "Just bring yourself; you are better than any medicine." They both laughed. "Stuart, tell your mum, I've met another dancer." He looked across at her.

"I suppose you will be teaching your daughter to dance."

Suddenly shy, Broyooy said, "…Maybe."

"Ginty would love that, but with two boys." He shrugged.

"Is that your wife?" He threw his head back and laughed.

"I'm foot loose and fancy free, sweetheart." He waved, blew them a kiss and went, winking at the nurse passing him in the door. Helen filled her in with the relationship. Now it was feeding time.

Helen explained to James the next time he came in about Bryony. Stuart did come again, but this time, there were flowers and chocolate for both of them. They would both be going home in three days and they had exchanged addresses and would visit in the near future. Helen thought Katriana would like Bryony, a lot.

The countryside was lush and green as the maroon Rover made its way to the lodge. An excited Angus and Mary greeted Helen and the new baby, entering the lodge, Helen found David and Lucinda Balentine from the Big House inside, all smiles. It was a lovely feeling and Helen watched their faces as they gazed at her son.

Mary sat holding the baby as Angus beamed alongside her. "Och, you made a good job of him, lass; he's a fine laddie." Angus's smile broadened even more; he was pleased there was new blood in the glen. Lucinda came over and hugged her.

"He's beautiful, James Junior," she said smiling at Helen and Mary. "I'm pleased it's over for you, Helen dear; it was a labour of love."

Two hours later, they made for the castle. We are home now, JJ; but he didn't want to wake up. One of the workers ran and opened the first gate for her and smiled at the sleeping baby. Then walked to the second gate, pulling the creaking iron structure. The gates were there now to make it harder for intruders and the prize bulls had been brought nearer the house for the last few years, but they had still lost Out of the Blue.

Andrew and Ginty's children were the first out, jumping about with excitement. Molly came hurrying out, and with the children calmed, she held JJ while Helen's chauffeur Lewis collected her belongings. Once inside the castle, Ginty and Molly's new helper came into the warm lounge, which was already prepared with a cot and tea and cakes. Katriana came in looking flushed. "Helen, it's good to have you home again, let me have a look at my new grandson." Helen removed one of his blankets revealing the pink cheeks and dark hair of the sleeping baby.

"Do you want to sit down, and I'll hand him to you." Sitting and holding her arms out, with the children coming for a closer look, Helen handed JJ to her.

"It's James all over again. Oh, how wonderful." She kissed him lightly on the cheek and smiled at the onlookers.

It still felt strange calling the castle home, but later that afternoon, James Senior was settled in an armchair with his new son in his arms. A picture of peaceful relaxation. Now that his wife and son were home, he felt all was right with his world. Looking at him, Helen felt true happiness, even though she thought he looked a little strained and tired and guessed the worry of the rustlers were to blame. They had two more men now working for them, which had made life a bit easier. He looked up at her. "Helen, I love you so much, thank you for this little bundle of joy."

James Junior turned out to be a contented baby and each day looked more like his father. His eyes, chin and expression were so alike. Two months later,

Helen sent her chauffeur to get Bryony and her daughter, taking them first to the lodge where Helen and the baby had been dropped off. Helen took a few photos of Mary holding the baby girl and Angus with JJ in his arms; they looked so happy. She sighed quietly to herself, knowing she missed living at the lodge. The castle was impressive, and she was, sort of, happy there.

Bryony looked very well and her daughter Lynette was dainty perfection with her white blonde hair, pale complexion and sky blue eyes. Molly had said she will be breaking a few hearts later on. At the castle, the women went into raptures over her; Ginty said she was now broody after seeing the baby girl. Poor Bryony was a little taken aback suddenly visiting a castle but soon adjusted to the surprise. Just before Bryony left, Stuart arrived back. His usual self-being really pleased to see them all there and rushing up to his quarters and quickly washing and changing. "Right, who's first?" he said picking up JJ and talking to him like a grownup. "He's a Mcklinross all right, your mum feeding you enough; now, I don't want any nonsense like crying three in the morning. I'm your favourite Uncle Stuart. Mother, would you like to hold your grandson?" He passed the baby to her. "Right, who's next, little princess, we've met before my angel, haven't we?" He lifted her out of her mother's arms to Bryony's astonishment and walked slowly around the room talking sweetly to her.

Going over to Bryony and smiling down at her, he said, "Well, she's got her mother's good looks." Bryony and Helen looked at each other as Helen winked. This turned out to be the first of many visits to the castle and the lodge for Bryony, and Stuart had taken a genuine liking to mother and baby. With all the willing babysitters, it was easy to arrange an evening out together. The six of them had become firm friends.

Chapter 23

It was becoming a frequent event for the men to collect in the castle grounds now, ready to start their search for rustlers. The children watched as the men rode out, their hooves echoing. James Junior now a tall three-year-old, stood with his cousins Duncan and Robert as they said some of the horses' names. "Daddy's is Cavalier, Uncle Stuart's is Grenadier." James Junior's voice was full of excitement. The boys pointed to one of the stockman's black horse, in unison said, "Warrior."

As they began to move off, Helen saw James, as he always did, turn in the saddle and blow them a kiss. Reading his silent words, 'see you later, love you'. They stood waiting until the hoof beats faded away.

Ginty and a stable hand came across the courtyard with two sets of saddles and bridles for Duncan and Robert to get their ponies ready to ride. "Is that right that Daddy is going to buy you a pony, JJ?" Helen asked jingling a bridle at him. Looking up at his mother, his face lit with happiness.

"Yes, and he asked me what colour I wanted." Now he had everyone's attention. The boys were eager to know more.

Uncle Andrew showed me a book with lots and lots of ponies. They all waited patiently. "So which one did you like?"

He was silent for a moment, then clapping his hands and laughing, said, "All of them."

After saddling up and mounting, they lifted James J up behind Duncan and took him for a ride around the castle grounds. "We will have to speed up the riding lessons, JJ, so we can all ride together."

"Auntie Helen, will Uncle James let us come with you to choose a pony?"

"Of course, every one." Helen smiled to herself; this was going to be fun and would probably take all day, still, time for ice cream and milkshakes and sweets.

The men had arrived at the rocky outcrop that seemed to be suspended in air. From here, they would be able to see almost the whole area and pick up on any movement below.

James went out onto the flat, stony grass area he had called his and Helen's favourite place and put his binoculars to his eyes. The men followed, the horses picking their way carefully. The air was still up here, but below them, the tops of trees were moving like waves on the sea. There was no visible clue as to where the rustlers would be hiding out and so many contours to hide among.

The men decided to move on. James stood taking a last look; Cavalier looked magnificent as did the man on his back. There was a flash and a crack of gunfire rang out from far below. Cavalier screamed in pain and reared up with a spurt of blood coming from his shoulder; stumbling backwards, he toppled over the precipice. To the men's horror, James was – thrown out of the saddle and disappeared over with him.

Dismounting, they scrambled to the edge. Stuart was screaming his brother's name, but there was no sign of horse or rider, just the sound of a few stones rolling down the hillside. David Balentine was shouting to Stuart. "Come on, man, we've got to get to lower ground and search, try to remember where the gunfire came from."

Hours later, they returned to the castle, dusty and downhearted. By this time, police and volunteers had started a search party. They found the body of Cavalier and buried him along with his saddle and bridle, but they dug the bullet out of his shoulder first in case it was evidence, but they couldn't find James.

Lewis walked away from the Rover and into the stables. He had his hands clasped over his ears. Tears rolled down his pale face.

Stuart stood holding Helen tight as she screamed uncontrollably at the sad news. A long time later, Helen asked Lewis to take her to the lodge, leaving James Junior with Mary and Angus. Lewis confided in them that he wasn't happy with Helen's plans to go and look for James but would stay with her and carry out her wishes. A shocked Mary was struggling to hold back the tears as Angus took James Junior and went out. It was obvious the little boy didn't know yet.

Mary dropped into a chair with her head in her hands. "Dear God, let this be a nightmare I will wake up from." Helen swayed a little and Lewis slipped his arm around her.

"Sit down for a minute, Helen." He started to pull a chair towards her, but she shook her head, placing a hand on Mary's shoulder with a helpless look and walked to the door.

Lewis wasn't happy about what she was about to do but drove her to the lower ground that would enable them to get near the stone outcrop a mere speck in the sky. As he put the brake on, Helen made to jump out of the car; he put his arm across and held her arm. He was upset seeing Helen like this. Turning a distraught face to him, he said, "I have to do this. I know he's here somewhere, Lewis." He removed his arm and vowed to himself he would do his utmost to help her regardless.

Helen scrambled wildly amongst the undergrowth calling James's name until she was so tired she sat down and cried. He saw some blood on her trousers and carefully lifted the bottom up, removing an ugly thorn. Helen had been searching for five hours. Looking up at the culprit outcrop, he didn't know how anybody could survive that drop, apart from all the jagged rocks sticking out on the way down. A large patch of freshly dug soil marked the spot that Cavalier now lay. Lewis would remember the fine figure of James on Cavalier for a long time.

"Please, Mrs McKlinross, let me take you back to the lodge." Helen looked at him, expressionless. "We can come back tomorrow at first light. We won't stop looking."

He handed her over to Angus who sat in the big armchair and cuddled her like he used to when she was young. While she sobbed quietly Mary and Lewis bathed her cuts and scratches and removed spiteful thorns. Helen looked up at Angus. "I know he's out there somewhere, Angus." He wiped her eyes. A slight hysteria sound had crept into her voice. "I've got to find him. I must find him."

James Junior appeared in the doorway rubbing his eyes; Mary went to him. "Oh, you're awake, my little man." Mary picked him up; turning around, his eyes grew large.

"Mummy, what's the matter?" Wriggling to get down, he also climbed onto Angus's lap and cuddled his mother.

A month later, the search parties stopped going out. Then one day, months later, a herdsman turned up at the lodge to speak to Angus. "As an old friend, I just want you to come with me so as there's no mistake and see what my old eyes think they can see. I nay want the lasses upset more, in case it's no."

Angus confirmed that it was definitely a body wedged between a slim gap in two rocks fairly high up. A team of men recovered the body, and James was brought home for burial.

Sitting in the castle nursery, Helen watched her son quietly lining up his toy tractor and jeep. The empty hopeless loneliness she felt made her body ache and the void in their lives without James was almost intolerable. Closing her eyes, silent tears rolled down her cheeks again. Every night as she climbed into her lonely bed, she didn't think she had any tears left.

Feeling her son curl his fingers into her hand, reminding her instantly of his father's touch, as kneeling close to her, he laid his head on her lap. Stroking his dark hair, * her hand touched his soft cheek letting her fingers follow the contours of his neck; she thought now of the unborn children that might have been. Silently she said, "Oh, James, why did you leave us, how could you?" she knew the words did not comfort.

Looking down at her son's dark head through rainbow tears, he was his father's image. The hollow deepened inside her. How was she going to go on, her love for him was immeasurable. Sudden cold loneliness engulfed her, she felt like snatching up her son and running away to the lodge to hide from the world.

Dabbing her tears and making a supreme effort to pull herself together, she knew everyone was suffering. Katriana was in a bad state of shock and her sister Silvana was on her way from Russia to take her back for a while, after the funeral. This had been a second family death for her to cope with and had sent her spiralling down into depression.

Stuart had been very quiet and went about his day's work noiselessly, beginning to look a little haggard. This terrible accident had affected everyone. The letters and cards of condolence came daily. James had been so respected and loved.

When thinking like this, she felt a rage inside her deepening; she would hunt the rustlers herself, knowing it to be impractical but thinking she would go to her and James's rocky outcrop one day and keep watch.

Helen decided to have James buried in their honeymoon cleit that he had prepared so beautifully in the shieling country for the first night of their marriage, telling her it will be our secret hideaway when life gets a bit hectic. Remembering with great clarity every wonderful moment. They had visited it on many occasions and the memory burned brightly inside her, knowing now it would last her a lifetime.

After dropping James Junior off at the lodge into the waiting arms of Angus and an excited Mary, Helen made her way to the shieling country. As the familiar countryside came into view, a sadness came with it.

Pulling into the side of the track, Helen sat there for a moment knowing she shouldn't have come alone, but she thought she heard voices, and who did the vehicle belong to she had seen further up the track? Venturing into the shrubbery that opened up to the rocky outcrop, she stopped suddenly and froze. There was someone already there, and she could hear a man's voice.

Fingering her collar, she drew out one of Aunt Matty's long lethal hatpins that had proved a great deterrent in London when she had to walk home from a performance late at night; she was ready to use it if she had to. Backing her way out, she stopped. The man's voice was familiar, punctuated with sobs.

Walking out onto the open rocky outcrop where her and James loved and lived so many happy memories, now the place where he lost his life, a cold shudder past over her as she saw it was Stuart in a state of despair. "James, James, my dearest brother, we could have let them have the bull...it's not worth a life." Heart broken, his words were interspersed with sobs.

Helen watched with an aching heart, not sure what to do for the best. Her own sorrow pushed to the back of her mind for the moment. To see a man cry was very upsetting, hearing him mention James's name and his father's. "We struggled to go on without you, Father, but I can't go on now without my brother – I can't, I can't." His voice trailed off into sobs, which shook his whole body, and he sank to his knees.

Helen went and stood beside him. "I'll help you, Stuart; we will help each other." He turned his tear-stained swollen eyes towards her, shaking his head.

"I can't go on." Sinking back on to his heels, his head bowed.

"We've got to; we'll make your father and James proud." Putting a comforting arm around him, his shoulders and arms limp, she felt the depth of his misery as the silent sobs shook his body.

"Stuart, don't cry anymore; come back with me," she said helping him up. "We will get through this." They clung on to each other making their way back to the cars. Stuart sat in his rough terrain car staring straight ahead. Helen sat with him for a while, worried he wasn't really in a fit state to drive himself safely.

After a while, he assured her he would be all right and put his hands on her shoulders.

"I'm grateful to you, Helen, my precious sister-in-law." They looked into each other's eyes for a long moment. "Yes, we will get through this," he said pulling her towards him and firmly hugging her.

Worrying all the way on the journey home and trying to put her own grieving to the back of her mind. Thinking perhaps it was worse for Stuart, he had lost his father when he was ten, thinking James was twelve when she first met him on the shieling move into the high ground. Pulling into the lodge, she sat for a few moments. It had been quite traumatic seeing Stuart on the outcrop in such a state. Later, she confided to Angus. "Aye, the lad is suffering." That evening, Angus took himself to the castle.

Chapter 24

The large statue, copied from one of her drawings of Cavalier, had now been put where the horse was buried. The granite blocks that formed the platform for him to stand on made it even more impressive.

On her bad days, she would drive out here and sit on the platform, alone with her memories and thoughts. Today, she sat here feeling the lush greenery in the glen wrapping itself around her.

As the ground rose, it gave way to sparse areas of grassland. Further up, the trees thinned out. Helen would not let herself look up finding it too painful. Perhaps one day.

Studying the hooves at close range, remembering how, on the banks of the burn Cavalier came almost up to her, seeing again her reflection in his eyes, could feel his breath as he lowered his head to pull the grass at her feet and see so plainly, James astride him looking down at her, the slight lift to the corner of his mouth; he was so clear in her mind's eye.

Again the feeling of loneliness engulfed her; she felt so sad and lost without him but so full of love. Her breath shuddered, but she wasn't going to let herself cry after all; she had been blessed with a son. Feeling something brush past her knee, opening her eyes slowly, she looked around without moving. All seemed quiet and undisturbed. Not wanting to move from this precious space. Sighing, she stood up. Closing her eyes again for a moment, she knew she had experienced this feeling before. Opening them, out of the corner of her eye, in the distance she thought she saw something white, wishing she had brought the binoculars.

Smiling and whispering under her breath, 'Lilly' but knowing Lilly wouldn't have left her hillside, but it was a warm feeling. Breathing deeply and suddenly feeling better, she made her way back to the car. In her mind, she could see James up on Cavalier, so clearly and knew what she was going to do.

James Junior was finishing his tea with the others but was very sleepy. Carrying him to the bedroom, he was already almost asleep.

Helen decided to go to bed as well. Tucking James Junior into his single grownup bed next to hers, she bent over him; his eyes looking at her without flinching. "Is there anything you would like, my darling?" He lay motionless.

After what seemed a long moment, he said, "I would like to kiss Daddy goodnight." Closing his eyes, he turned over, knowing his wish would go unfulfilled and experiencing that empty hollow that now lived deep inside him.

Trying to read a book, her concentration was poor. So much kept crowding into her mind. Looking through the book cabinet half-heartedly, there was a tap on her door. Stuart came to say good night. "Is he asleep yet?" She shook her head. "Can I say goodnight to the little man?" Helen could hear their quiet chatter; she noticed how Stuart had lost weight, but funnily, it suited him. He came with a smile and stood beside her. "Are you all right…" Then he gently hugged her. "We are bearing up…" His hug took on a slight rocking movement.

Later, putting her book away and still feeling Stuart's hug, it had been comforting. Just about to turn the light out, her son turned over; she waited.

Restless and his eyes full of worry, he sat up. Blinking, he asked, "Mummy, can I come in your bed with you?" Flicking the bedclothes back, suddenly brought a warm memory of her and James on Fay Island when she was afraid.

Smiling, she replied, "Jump in darling." He was soon snuggled into her and sleeping soundly. Helen lay motionless, happier memories floating about her, filling the large room. Sleep wasn't far off. This little scrap lying close to her had been made with love by her and James; she knew it was one of the greatest loves ever known and was proud.

The castle lounge was quiet this afternoon. Lewis, Helen's chauffeur, worried about her, suggested that Bryony and her daughter come over for the afternoon. Seeing her smile and nod her agreement, he had collected them. As the two women talked quietly, James Junior and Lynnette played with a wooden farm set at the other end of the lounge talking amicably interspersed with Lynnette's gentle tinkling laughter. "See, this is my field with my horse." Standing a little brown horse in the middle.

"Would you like a horse?" He erected another field; she looked at him and smiled.

"But where would it live?"

"In this field next to mine." They both laughed.

Looking at them, Helen thought as always this little girl was good for her son; she managed to lift his darkness. Turning to Bryony she said, "So why is it necessary for you to leave your flat?"

"It's complicated, but in a nutshell, my landlord has given notice to all four flats because he wants to sell the property, actually, he tells us it is now as good as sold."

"Oh, Bryony, six weeks isn't long."

Shrugging, she said, "I'm looking around, something will turn up. I've already seen two, but one didn't want children and the other was too far away." Helen's brain was working overtime; no way did she want this precious friend to fade from her life.

A little burst of laughter caught their attention. "What are you two up to?"

James, all smiles, said, "Her horse has jumped out of his field." Pointing and laughing, lighting up her face. "Now he's jumped back again." More laughter. Bryony was getting ready to leave, holding out a light pink coat to Lynnette.

"Thanks for a nice afternoon, Helen, see you again soon."

James Junior climbed up to the window and watched them go, his mood noticeably changing. Starting to put the farm animals back into the toy box, he asked, "Can Lynnette come again tomorrow, Mum?" Helen knew she would be putting a suggestion to the rest of the family tonight.

By the end of the week, Bryony and Lynnette were happily settled into their own quarters in the castle. Everyone gave a hand and poor Bryony had a few tears at their kindness. Helen smiled as James Junior helped carry some of Lynnette's belongings. Something new happening had helped take their minds off the approaching burial.

Chapter 25

On the day of James's funeral, Helen felt her movements were mechanical, moving in a dream state as if she would wake up soon and this terrible business over. A few people were arriving so she made her way to the kitchen. Angus was there, and Mary and Molly had taken charge of the two young children James Junior and Lynnette.

At the start of the well-trodden path, there were lots of cars being parked and a long procession of people were forming and slowly making their way to where the mounds started. Helen found herself holding on Angus's arm and losing herself in thought of when she and James walked this road, and he explained to her about the mounds. As the road gradually curved, looking back, the sight of the procession of people seem to stretch for miles. As she watched, seeing people here and there placing stones on the mounds of loved ones, gave her comfort.

Now at the cleit, it stood wide open. The old bed of bracken and heather was gone. The bed James had shown her so much love and passion on, memories crowded about her.

Watching the coffin being slid into the right side of the cleit, its last resting place and the entrance now being secured, Helen knew that one day she would lay alongside James, and it felt right.

On the way down now to where the many cars had been parked as Helen looked about, it seemed unreal. It was all over. There were so many familiar faces, and Helen told herself that she must get around to thanking them all. Later, although a sad occasion, David and Lucinda had been in their element welcoming everyone into Eagle Place. Gentle chatter filled the ballroom, and around the walls were tables full of food. Looking at Andrew, Stuart and Angus in there tartans, she felt a sense of pride. Everyone made a blanket of colour that wrapped itself around her. James Junior slipped his hand into hers. "Is Daddy there now, Mummy?" Stroking his velvety black hair and looking into his young innocent eyes, so trusting.

"Yes, darling. We will go to the cleit one day, just you and me."

"And Lynnette." She looked at the two young children in their kilts that Stuart had bought them, knowing it was good for James to have this valued little friend.

"Of course, dear." Somehow, the little girl's presence seemed to ease things for her son.

Stuart seemed to be coping and he and Bryony had shadowed Katriana. Andrew, Ginty and their two sons were a credit to the family standing tall and looking colourful in their tartans and working hard at mixing. Helen took the opportunity to introduce the boys to the Nicholson girls. They remembered the story of the goats and chickens.

Finding an inner strength, she managed to get through the day. She talked to her friends from Fay Island, Hamish and Megan and the twins, now tall and sturdy young men. She smiled as she saw the lady from Shoreside Refreshments adding some food to the tables and recognising some of the tenant farmers she had visited on occasions. A group of her dance friends came over, hugging her. They were staying with Angus and Mary, who had told them a long time ago to treat the lodge as their second home but wishing it was a happier occasion. They made Helen promise to come to London, and she felt it would be a good idea. Claudette linked arms with her. "You coming to London, Helen; we would like to know a date before we go; we've got a nice place for you to stay."

Squeezing her arm, Claudette extracted a promise and a rough date. They all felt it might do her good. Tito announced he had already told James Junior they would be going to the big London zoo. "He wants the little song bird to come as well." Helen looked puzzled, then realised he meant Lynnette.

The lady from one of the farmsteads that had given her the goats and chickens asked her how she was getting on with them. Helen told her the truth that she had someone else looking after them, and they had done very well at some shows, which pleased her, and she introduced them to the Nicholsons to tell her more about it. The girls were excited to find someone so interested in their goats, and she was going to call in on her way home.

At the breakfast table, all had left except Ginty who was now going through her flower press box and Lynnette. Her mum Bryony had gone to collect some washing together.

Ginty smiled at her then carefully inspected some very small flowers noticing the little girl looking at her intently as she slowly spooned her breakfast cereal.

"Enjoying that, Lynnette?" She nodded as she carried on eating still looking at Ginty. Noticing traces of tears beginning as she put her spoon down, she went over to her and picked her up, sitting her on her lap.

"What's the matter, darling?" she asked wiping her tears. "Don't you feel very well?" Lynnette swallowed hard in an attempt not to cry. Without blinking,

"James J cried this morning."

"Sweetheart." She cuddled the child to her feeling her delicate frame, so different to her well-built boys. "Yes, I know, dear, we are all a bit sad at the moment, but we have to be very grown up and strong." The large eyes looked up at her.

"I miss Uncle James too, but I don't want JJ to cry."

Ginty rocked her gently. "We all miss Uncle James," she said sighing. Not really knowing what to say to the little girl to comfort her. "We will all meet again."

"Where?"

"A long time in the future yet, but in heaven." Smiling down at her, Ginty added, "We are all going to heaven one day." Lynnette sat up and looked at her with large innocent eyes.

"Is that where Uncle James is now."

Smiling, Ginty replied, "Yes."

"Why do they call you Ginty?" It was something she had wanted to ask for a long time.

Pleased to see a lift in the girl's mood she explained, "I have a brother and when he was small he couldn't get his tongue around my proper name Geanette; he always called me Ginty and so did everyone else then." Lynnette was smiling now.

Climbing down she said, "I really like you, Ginty and Auntie Helen." Leaving the room, she stopped at the door, looking back, smiled and was gone.

Speaking to the empty space Ginty said, "I like you too, Lynnette." She was still able to feel her against her body. Her boys were the world to her and Andrew, but the little girl had felt like a breath of spring. Taking a deep breath, she turned her attention to her flower press.

The water lapped slowly over the fine shingle at the edge of the lake. Helen and Bryony watched their children splashing about, both could swim, their wet suits shining as they stood up laughing, plunging out of sight, popping up somewhere else. Lost in memory, Helen saw once again her and James enjoying the waterfalls in shieling times and for a few moments, closing her eyes, she relived the happiness.

Helen had been surprised at Bryony's knowledge of old Edinburgh although she did rent a flat near the university. "The city has a reputation for research in medicine; there's the Royal College of Surgeons followed by Royal College of Physicians and later the School of Medicine. Oh, I could go on all day; the city's medical history is incredible. You would find the Surgeons Hall Museum very interesting; it's on Nicolson Street. Although thinking about it, you might find the Festival Theatre more to your taste, that's on the same street. Some of the history is gruesome."

Bryony and Lynnette now lived at the castle and Helen, Ginty and Katriana enjoyed having them there, especially when Katriana brought out her photos and they could all lose themselves in the dance world. Feeling a few cold droplets, Helen realised the children had come out of the water.

Now in the warmth of the kitchen, everyone's favourite place, tucked into crusty rolls spreading thick butter, ham and mustard, then dipping chocolate biscuits into their hot drinks. The children now warmly dressed took themselves off to the stables just as Andrew and Stuart came in. "The boys are in the stables," Andrew informed them. "If you go out, no galloping." Stuart gave both girls an affectionate kiss on the cheek.

Bryony looked at Stuart's back disappearing through the door and sighed. Looking at Helen she said, "I did love my husband." Helen looked at her. "I thought he loved me, love is very fickle." She sat thinking. "Do you know, it's strange, but after he went, I felt nothing but relief, just think, if he hadn't decided to go, I would have missed all this. I feel blessed at our paths crossing in the hospital." Smiling, she left the table.

The weather was disappointing. Lynnette and James Junior were in the main lounge and the log fire was alight making a cosy atmosphere. From the kitchen, singing and laughter from the lounge could be heard, so Andrew and Ginty's boys Duncan and Robert went to investigate. Opening the door and peeping in saw a happy scene; they stood watching for a few moments, then decided to join them.

Stuart was sitting on the floor with some books and papers. The children were asking for Stuart to do The Laughing Policeman again. 'Ive not got enough puff left, all that laughing, what about - Nellie the Elephant' - and started singing. They all joined in followed by – Teddy Bear's Picnic and The Runaway Train.

When they had calmed down from laughing, Stuart picked up a colourful comic book. "I'm going to read you a story." Getting up, he made himself comfortable on the long sofa with one either side of him and the boys in the armchairs. "Ready…This is the story of a cowboy called Roy Rogers and his horse Trigger."

"Did he have to ride the boundaries like Daddy did?" James Junior's eyes were wide with interest. Stuart wondered for a moment whether he had chosen the right sort of story. Although inside he was crying and his heart was breaking, he decided to go on with the story.

"You see, he lived in a far off land and him and Trigger used to hunt baddies." Lynnette sat forward.

"What colour was his horse."

"Beautiful, a very light brown gold and his mane and tail were white. He had very unusual light-coloured hooves, but he could gallop as fast as the wind. One day…"

By the afternoon, the weather was a full-blown storm, despite this a visitor had turned up at the castle wanting to see Katriana and Helen. Katriana showed her into the lounge. "It's a long time since I've seen you, Ruth. How are you?" Nervously twisting a handkerchief, she gave her condolences for James.

"I saw him at Fay Island when I went to the conference about the new observatory that's going to be built over there. I'm so glad I saw him, I…" Wiping her eyes and dabbing her nose, she continued, "Sorry. Is it possible for me to have a word with James's wife?"

Andrew and Ginty's eldest son Duncan came to tell Helen that Katriana wanted to see her in the main lounge. "Thank you, Duncan; I'll be down in a minute." She had been busy looking through some papers of James. Duncan hesitated.

"There's a visitor downstairs." So Helen put the lid on the box she had been sorting through and they went down together.

Entering the hallway and looking towards the lounge, the door was open and Helen could see a woman talking to Katriana. Although she had her back to her, Helen was in no doubt who it was. It was redheaded Ruth. Helen stopped; she was in no mood to see this woman and began to turn around. Katriana called to her, and Helen carried on into the lounge politely saying hallo. Ruth looked at her, and there was no disguising she had been crying, her eyes were red and swollen and her make up a little spoilt.

Katriana stood up patting Ruth's arm and came over to Helen. "Ruth would like to talk to you," she said looking at her purposefully with a faint smile. "I'll just go and arrange some tea for us." As the door closed quietly, Ruth turned towards Helen. The two women faced each other for an awkward few seconds. Taking a hankie from her bag, she wiped her eyes and face.

"I feel I owe you an explanation for my behaviour towards James." Collecting herself and taking a shuddering breath, she continued, "There was never anything between James and me. I admit I had a crush on him in college and we were good friends; we worked on the observatory project in the same group." She folded her hankie and tucked it neatly into her handbag. "But he was never interested in me, not like I was with him."

Helen thought it was time she sat down. Now looking at the young woman, she felt sorry for her; she had obviously been very fond of James, and their friendship went back a long way. Then musing in her thoughts, not as long ago as hers. Helen noticed her glancing at the drinks table. "Would you like a drink?" she asked indicating the table. "Our hot drink seems to have gone astray."

Moving to the table. "A drop of whisky would be welcome."

Pouring it, Helen felt she might benefit from one herself. Handing Ruth her glass and sitting down again, the two women sipped their drinks looking at one another. "Ruth, there was never an issue between James and me; you were a little forward, but I'm not a jealous person and I trusted James; we loved each other very much; you have nothing to reproach yourself about; we've both lost him." Ruth visibly relaxed; finishing her drink, she sat with her hands in her lap.

"What are you going to do, Helen?" Raising her head slowly, taking a last sip, she replaced her glass quietly.

Looking directly into Ruth's eyes, Helen replied, "I'm going to hunt out the person that did this, and I'm going to kill him myself."

Although taken aback for a moment, it wasn't what she had expected her to say. Ruth was totally unperturbed. "I'll help you." The door opened and Katriana came in with the maid bearing a tray.

Over the coming weeks, the two women came to know each other well. It seemed Ruth knew a lot of people, possibly in the line of work, as she did the books for the management at the cattle market in Edinburgh, that might be able to shed some light or information without raising suspicion. It was a start, and as time went on, their circle grew bigger adding Ginty and Bryony. The four of them formed a tight bond of friendship and met often for coffee and to exchange ideas.

Lewis brought the car to the kitchen door in readiness to drive Helen to Edinburgh. He stood holding the door open for her and felt the same worry pop into his head. To his surprise, she motioned she wanted to sit in the front with him. Lewis settled her in the front and started the car. A sideways glance told him she was smiling, which made him smile too. This was something new; he had never known her travel in the front and enjoyed the close proximity.

In Edinburgh. "Where would you like me to stop?" He brought the car to a slow standstill a few yards from the impressive white building that housed the specialists. Keeping his voice level, he said, "I hope all is well with you." Helen smoothed her hair back and buttoned her coat. He opened the door and waited. On the pavement, she turned looking at him, her faithful chauffeur whom she had great faith in and trusted.

"It's only a check-up." Turning away, she took a few steps, stopped, then turned. Looking at him, still holding the door, worry lines creased his forehead. "We will talk when I come back." He watched her walk away, so he had stopped in the right place.

An hour later, he had driven her to the top of candle maker Row so that they could have lunch in the historical 'Greyfriars Bobby' teashop made famous in the mid-Victorian times by an extraordinary dog who had kept vigil on his master's grave for fourteen long years. Helen looked about the quaint teashop with its many cards and a statue of the black Scottish dog sitting patiently on a pedestal, thinking she would buy some cards of Greyfriars Bobby for her dance friends; they would love the story.

Helen sat back heaving a contented sigh as their dishes were cleared away. The starter had been a warming bowl of lobster bisque, followed by Scottish poached salmon, creamy mashed potato, whipped mustard cream and peas, sweet and tender, just like Angus grew. Patting her tummy, she said, "The desserts look lovely, but I couldn't manage one." She dabbed the corners of her mouth with the serviette and smiled. Lewis sat forward and studied her.

"Don't think me presumptuous but you did say we would talk when you came away from…" He pulled nervously at his cuffs.

Helen lowered her eyes, then looked up smiling. "Yes, I did and as I said, it was only a check-up. The doctor wants to keep an eye on me. It seems I have two leaky heart valves now." Her smile broadened. "Not satisfied with one. I have two." Then she managed an attractive laugh. "Lewis, your face is a picture. It's nothing to worry about; it's all under control." Then in a more serious tone, she said, "It's just between you and me. I don't want anyone worrying for nothing." Lewis closed his mouth and swallowed hard, now he knew. It had set a small alarm bell ringing in his head and knew his worries had been confounded.

Holding the door and watching her walk through to the breezy outside, he thought how lovely she looked and how much he had enjoyed being with her. Helen paused looking at the cards she had just purchased. "My dance friends will love these." Helen slipped her arm through his. "You don't mind me holding your arm, do you, Lewis; it feels more comfortable." Lewis felt ten feet tall and took off his chauffeur's hat and slipped it under his arm.

Arriving at the castle among lots of excitement, she was just in time to see Out of the Blue being unloaded. Duncan and Robert ran to meet her car. "Auntie Helen our champion bull has come home; the policeman had a great big photo."

"Yes, the one you took on Fay Island." The two boys were glowing with excitement. They all stood watching the slow process as the bull was now an old man and much slower but just as magnificent.

Chapter 26

Ginty found the kitchen empty this afternoon, so she collected her flower press tweezers and glue, setting them out on the table went out to collect an array of dainty greenery and tiny colourful flowers. Unscrewing the four corners of the press, she noticed for some reason she had built more padding into one of the sections so carefully removed the wooden squares. Horror struck, her hands flew to her cheeks. There, sitting neatly in its cushioned centre in perfect condition was the rose that James had asked her to press for him. The rose he had carried in his pocket next to his heart that had fallen from Helen's hair. He had confided in her his feelings for Helen and said that one day he would have it dipped in silver or gold.

Searching for her hankie, she stifled a sob. "Sorry, James, I completely forgot it was there. I should have told dear Helen." Replacing the contents of the flower press, it would have to wait for another day, she decided to find Helen and tell her. She hadn't thought about it when James died, the shock had blanked out a lot of things. Wiping her eyes and blowing her nose, feeling somehow she had let him down, she collected up her press and hurried through the door.

Andrew had returned with the boys in an excited state all talking at once. James Junior had fallen in love with a silver grey Welsh mountain pony, and it was being delivered later today. The boys were now all heading for the stables to prepare the bedding and feed in a hay net. Andrew had told James Junior he thought the pony was a lovely colour, the colour of the silver mist that rolled over the mountains. James Junior smiled at him knowing instantly that was going to be his name. "Thank you, Uncle Andrew," he said then took off like the wind. "I'm going to tell Mummy."

Hurrying into the castle, an excited James Junior found Ginty talking earnestly to her and waited quietly. Helen put her arm around Ginty. "It's the most wonderful present; thank you for looking after it." Ginty turned and hugged Helen.

"He loved you so much," she said stroking James Junior's hair as she passed him.

"Guess what, I have the most beautiful pony in the world, come and look, and he's six, the same age as Lynnette and me. Come on, and his name is Silver Mist of McKlinross."

Hurrying with James Junior to the stables, Helen saw that nearly everyone was there waiting. A little while later, the horsebox pulled slowly into the castle grounds and stopped. The excitement was palpable. Watching the two men let the rear of the horsebox down and lift the folding gate back, there was silence. Everyone waited, then a silver grey white head looked around the edge of the box, looking for the first time at his new home. One of the men walked him slowly and carefully down the ramp. Andrew took James's hand and went over to the new pony and put the halter rope in his hand. James Junior's face was a picture. "Mummy, look, this is Silver Mist, isn't he lovely? Do you like him?" Andrew picked him up and gently and quietly lowered him onto the pony's back. "Daddy would have loved him," he said leaning forward stroking his neck. Stuart came and stood alongside him with Lynnette on his shoulders.

"You are beautiful, Silver," Helen said as she reached down to stroke him. His smile couldn't get any wider.

Stuart went to where Bryony was standing. "Well, it seems we are a horsey family; we'd better get this young lady sorted soon; the boys will give her some lessons; don't look so worried, my lovely."

James Junior had no problem with riding, taking to it immediately, but Lynnette wasn't so sure, but she would give it a go. A month later, it was her turn to wait excitedly as the horsebox drove in. A pretty cream-coloured Palomino pony was led down the ramp, a flaxen blond mane and tail, almost the same colour as Lynnette's hair. "I'm going to call him Rupert." The boys teased her, telling her it was a bear's name. "Only in your comic," she said making them all laugh.

They all spent a lot of time in the stables but had to wait for the blacksmith to shoe Rupert and Silver before they could be ridden. Then lessons started in earnest, and James Junior and Lynnette were soon competent riders. The boys had worked hard and were pleased with the results; it had been easier than they had thought. Now they could look forward to riding out together. Fortunately, the horses all got on well with each other.

In the background, Lewis had been watching with interest and felt a proud admiration for the family's resilience. Although he worked for them and enjoyed his role, he would have loved to be a proper part of the family. Gradually, every one drifted away from the stables, but Helen paused watching the stable cat. Speaking softly and bending slowly to stroke the upturned face and arched back as it rubbed itself across her legs. Lewis noted once again, something that worried him as he saw Helen carefully place her hand across her chest then bend down. The worry niggle at the back of his brain popped up again, but then she looked up and smiled and he smiled back as she turned and walked across the spacious courtyard.

Sighing, Lewis carried on polishing the Rover. Helen had already told him she needed him to take her to Edinburgh at the beginning of next week; he felt it was something to look forward to.

Dusk wasn't far away, as the children rode into the castle grounds. The sun was very low in the sky now making the lake look the palest of gold. The reeds and shrubbery here and there a shadowy black making long thin fingers across the water. They sat quietly speaking in low whispers. Lynnette slipped the bag that had carried lunch off her shoulders finding a last chocolate bar and waited. Robert did the same, finding the remains of a roll. "Right, what shall we do about what we found?" Duncan being the eldest, felt responsible. Robert wasn't quite so sure.

"I don't think we should do anything at the moment. Let's keep it to ourselves for now." Dismounting, they went into the stables. It had been a long day and they had covered a lot of ground; they were tired, dusty and hungry.

An hour later seated around the table in the castle kitchen tucking into rabbit stew, they decided, as they were on their own, to have a discussion. They were all very fond of the castle cook; the food had changed slightly, but Molly seemed to approve, and there were no complaints from the men. James turned and smiled at the cook and saw her nod. Raising both arms in the air, he said, "Yes…Cooks, fruit crumble for dessert." They all started talking at once.

"Mary and Angus are coming over tonight," the cook informed them. They stopped talking, looking meaningfully at each other. The cook went out and

Duncan whispered, "That's what we'll do, talk it over with Angus. Your mum's out with redheaded Ruth doing her bit. See what Angus says, now, we do remember the exact place that's the most important thing?"

Ginty put her head around the door. "Ah, the happy wanderers, have a nice ride." Lots of nodding heads as the crumble finished up. "You were out a long time; are you finished in the stables?" More nodding heads. "Good, you can get washed and changed; we have company tonight." This time the heads went from side to side, then there was laughter.

Later that evening, with Angus cleverly way laid, the four of them told him what they had found and what was the best thing to do.

Telling Angus they wanted to show him the new ponies, they made their way to the stables, recently converted from one of the old bullpens. Now having Angus all to themselves, they sat down on the already arranged bales of straw that Duncan had prepared. Silver Mist and Rupert had their heads over the bar and were watching with great interest.

Thoughtfully stroking one of the muzzles, Angus asked, "Now what's this all about?" The group looked at Duncan.

"If you don't mind, Angus, we'd like some advice." He looked at the four innocent looking faces and smiled to himself, studying them for a moment.

"What have you been up to then?" Angus asked and sat back and waited.

"We've found something that we think is to do with the rustlers." Angus sat forward, all ears now.

"What makes you think it's to do with the rustlers?"

"Well, we are almost sure that it's something they constructed and it's not all that far away."

"Well, laddie, let's go and have a look," he said, taking his car key out. A tinkling laugh escaped from Lynnette.

"You can't drive there."

"No, you have to ride there," explained James Junior. "You would never see it from a car."

"So where exactly is it or what is it?" They all began talking at once. Duncan held his hand up and they were quiet.

"It's one of the tallest trees on the hillside, and it has an almost invisible ladder right to the top. I went right up and I'm telling you, with good binoculars you can see right into the castle grounds, almost into the bullpens, and further into the distance, you can see into the Big House, even your lodge, with binoculars of course. We don't know what to do about it." They sat looking at Angus. "Really, we shouldn't have been up on the high hillside, Dad and Uncle

Stuart don't like us on too higher ground, especially when we used to ride doubles." Robert thought it better to be honest.

Looking thoughtful, he said, "It's time to put the search party in the picture. You've been very observant and this place has to be made known to them." Angus stood up running his hand along the neck of one of the ponies and smiled at them.

"You won't be riding doubles anymore."

Since the discovery of the concealed ladder to the top of the giant Scotch pine tree, the men have had a meeting and have hatched a plan of action. It was decided that Andrew's son Duncan would show Stuart the place so as not to attract attention and then a trap would be set.

Angus visited the police station and had a private meeting with the chief constable that he knew there and put them in the picture as to what they were planning to do. They had kept it as secret as possible. A new champion bull would be acquired and the word put around about its pedigree to arouse interest. Its name would be entered in the next big cattle show, owners being McKlinross at Watersmeet Castle, then they would do a lot of movement around the bullpens where they knew they were being observed now. The next cattle show was the three counties big event in six weeks' time. All they had to do now was wait.

Duncan, Robert, James and Lynnette rode out together often but kept well away from the area of the ladder tree, as they referred to it now. There was an undeniable excitement between them, knowing what was going on but a secret.

For the last month, there had been some Romany Gypsies set up camp in the lower forest. "The Romany moved camp yesterday." James heard Robert's voice somewhere behind the straw bales as he cleaned his stirrup leathers. "I saw them heading south on the main road, the horse drawn caravans are really colourful." James fixed the stirrups back onto the saddle, giving the leathers a last wipe. "Yeah, they did cheer the place up." The boys walked together heading for the castle kitchen where a tempting smell of food beckoned. The cook had made two large lamb pies, and they stood steaming on the side of the oven and alongside them two fruit pies, making everyone's mouth water. They would soon be devoured as everyone started turning up.

A car arrived at the castle. James became curious as no one got out. Leaving his food for the moment, he went to see why, finding it was Angus's car. Angus and Mary made no attempt to get out, then, on the back seat, James saw a scruffy little dog. James put his head back in the kitchen. "Come and see what Angus and Mary have in their car."

James, Lynnette, Robert and Duncan all trooped out to see what the surprise was. Angus had the door open now, and as soon as Lynnette saw the little dog, she scooped it up in her arms. Mary's worried voice could be heard from inside the car. "Angus, the poor thing hasn't had a bath, and you're letting the wee one cuddle it."

"Will ye get out the car, woman, and go inside and explain."

They all fussed over the dog in the kitchen, putting a bowl of water down and getting the biscuit tin out. "He was just sitting by the roadside; I canna understand it; there's no one around for miles; it baffles me." The dog was now on James's lap with Lynnette stroking its scruffy head.

"Baffles, that's what we will call you, Baffles."

Duncan, Robert and James looked at each other. "The Romany Gypsies, they left yesterday."

"They either lost him or left him behind." Robert seemed so sure. Angus scratched his head.

"Aye, ye'ell no find em now." The cook put some leftover meat stew in a bowl; the little dog was certainly hungry.

"There's no problem is there…We can keep him…Can't we?" Duncan watched him lick the bowl clean. "That's nice, Baffles."

Stuart and Andrew were talking, then tapped the table for quiet. "Right, if the dog stays, you take it in turns to see it gets fed, clean water in its bowl, make up its bed and clean up its…dodos, is that understood? Applies to you four…er…Castle Cavaliers. He needs to go out in the grounds now that he's eaten. Well, off you go." They were laughing as they went out.

"Come on, Baffles, you've got to do – dodos." The little dog knew it was home and started wagging its tale.

In the lounge, the women were sipping tea. "Well, Katriana, that's another member of the family. I hope it's all right." Mary still sounded worried.

"It's perfectly all right; it doesn't look a problem," she said laughing good naturedly. "Our family has been increasing lately, and I find it…comforting." Mary smiled at her knowing exactly what she meant. "Only we didn't know what to do with it for the best. I am pleased you are taking in the poor wee thing." Putting her cup down, she said, "I hear you have ponies as well, and Molly is away visiting."

Helen walked with James and Lynnette then watched them mount and ride off at a fast trot. James Junior turned and waved, blowing her a kiss. She felt a cold hand snatch at her heart reminding her of the last time she saw his father alive. They were older and competent riders and would be meeting up with Duncan and Robert.

Walking back into the castle set her thinking; they weren't only good riders, now they were both becoming very good dancers with their classes at Mount Eagle Place. She wondered what her husband would have thought about his son dancing. Back in the castle kitchen, Stuart and Bryony looked up and smiled. Stuart was pouring more tea. "Come and sit down again, more tea, what about a coffee?" If she almost closed her eyes, it could have been James she was looking at and his memory filled her with love.

"No, thanks, I'm just going to make a phone call."

James and Lynnette had just reached Cavalier's grave. The statue was impressive. They both climbed up onto the large granite blocks and sat leaning on the statue's front legs, looking up under the horse's head. "Did you know that Cavalier was copied from a sketch my mum did?" She looked into the distance.

"Your mum's very clever. I saw her dance in the studio in Mount Eagle Place. It was lovely." Looking at James she said, "Do you know what I'd like? I'd really like to be able to dance like her one day." He was quiet for a while.

"You know what I'd like? What I'd really like? I'd like to look into the distance and see my father riding up to me on Cavalier. They were such a lovely sight." He stood up and jumped lightly down, holding his hands out for her, his voice was very quiet. "But I haven't got a father anymore." Lynnette took his hands, pausing, looked at him.

"I haven't a father either," she said jumping daintily down.

Duncan and Robert came up to them in a full gallop, their horses stopping expertly dispelling any sadness of the moment, their smiling faces pleased to share some cob nuts they had picked. "Robert nearly had a fall; he stood up on the horse to pick the nuts and over reached."

"Yes, but it was worth it." He pulled lots from his pockets, sharing them.

Chapter 27

Helen was not liking the feeling in her chest. It was like an angry moth banging itself against a light. Keeping still and breathing deeply, she thought about the dance school as a distraction. It had been an immediate success and the classes were filling up. The niggle remained.

The feeling had woken her again. She lay quiet in the dark, wide awake now, a deep burning sensation of mounting anger. Sighing, would this feeling ever leave her, she doubted it. James had been dead for several years now, but her decision to hunt his killer was just as strong now as in the beginning. The fact that Ruth was still by her side in the search, gave her hope. Several times, they felt they were near to finding the rustlers with promising clues but each time amounted to nothing in the end. Still they soldiered on.

At breakfast, there was a letter for her. Not recognising the handwriting, she opened it with mounting interest, noticing it was from Fay Island. Taking her coffee into the lounge, settling herself, she learned it was from Toby, the barman at the Sentinel, letting her know there had been some men staying that he was very suspicious of, especially one of them boasting about what a crack shot he was and could hit his target over any distance. Toby stressed that he was not a nice character and someone to be wary of. "Dear Helen, I have a suspicious feeling about this and know any clues helpful. I remember what James told us. I hope this might be helpful, but please be careful; let the police handle it." Helen smiled; the police hadn't been very helpful so far; they wanted evidence.

Putting the letter back in the envelope, she felt something else and pulled out a photo. Toby had obviously taken it in the bar, a big man with a cocky sneer. They are leaving on Friday and going back to Edinburgh. Studying the photo, she knew she hadn't seen this man before.

Going back into the kitchen, as Ginty and Bryony were on their own, she gave them the letter to read then went to phone Ruth. How kind of Toby. She trusted his judgement and would keep the photo in her handbag.

Ruth had driven over this afternoon in response to Helen telling her about Toby from the Sentinel's letter. There was an air of concentration as Helen, Ruth, Ginty and Bryony studied a map of the city of Edinburgh. The map was a large detailed one, and they had spread it over the round marble coffee table, of generous size and a centrepiece to the castle lounge.

Bryony was pointing out the area they had been talking about, although she wasn't very comfortable with the fact that Helen and Ruth wanted to go there. It was the old part of Edinburgh and had a reputation as a collecting place for crooks, thieves and the low and undesirable, a place where deeds were planned and deals made with a lot of money changing hands. Ruth sat up and was thoughtful. "Bryony, how come you know so much about this seedy area?" In her up front manner, she added, "If you don't mind me asking." Bryony sat back and took a deep breath, rubbing her back.

"Well, everything was all right at first, but then my husband started mixing with the wrong type of people. When I used to finish work, I would go looking for him. I knew where he would be. Mostly in 'The Black Moon' public house. It isn't a very nice place; I don't think you should go there."

Ruth looked apologetically at Bryony. "I didn't mean to pry, sorry." Bryony smiled at her and picked up her cup. "What about this other place?" Ruth wanted to know more now they were getting somewhere. The lounge door opened.

"Well, this is nice ladies; it's coffee time. Molly and the cook gone visiting and there's us workers gasping for a drink." Stuart tut-tutted as no one moved.

"More coffee for us, Stuart, made with hot milk, and can you bring in some of the cook's Dundee cake. We are a bit busy. Now, where were we?" The four of them smiled at each other, as Ginty's request seemed to work. Bryony sat forward and pointed to a thin line, hardly noticeable.

"This is the narrow lane almost running under part of the city I mentioned. It isn't very well known, but at this end is 'The Tickling Trout' public house, another no go area for you ladies. If you don't mind me saying, you two are going to stand out like a—"

To everybody's amazement, the coffee arrived.

They decided that it would be better to go to Edinburgh tomorrow. "Shall we leave at about six o'clock. I mean not a lot will be happening before that." Helen agreed that Ruth was right and not a lot would be happening before that, but the thought of being in a place like that as it was about to get dark didn't seem a good idea.

"What about starting off by having dinner in Edinburgh earlier and getting the feel of the place?" Ruth thought this a good idea and said they could meet at the 'Pleated Plaid'. "The food is good; it's on the Royal Mile; you can't miss it, just keep walking uphill."

Helen had put Lewis in the picture, as she wanted to be sure he would pick them up as soon as they had looked over the two shady pubs. He wasn't happy about the arrangement and offered to come with them, but Helen declined. "It isn't an area I am familiar with, but if you would drop me at one end of the Royal Mile, I could walk to the other end and look at the shops. Bryony says there are some really nice ones." Lewis took a while to answer.

"Are you sure you wouldn't like me to take you straight to the restaurant?" Helen shook her head.

Helen enjoyed the shops and the walk and was now looking for the Pleated Plaid Restaurant. Looking from side to side of the road, she saw Ruth already seated at a table. Having to walk down some red-carpeted steps, she could just see her in the corner.

After their salmon dinner and plum pudding sweet, they discussed their plan of action over a glass of white wine. Helen unrolled the map to the place where the narrow alley could just be seen. "Bryony did say that this would be mostly the back of places so perhaps we could slip in the back way when we find the pub without being noticed." Helen had to admire Ruth's way of thinking. "I don't think there is any chance of us not being noticed." Helen put on the scarf she had brought with a deliberate tear in and a pair of horn-rimmed glasses, pulling some hair onto her face, looking at Ruth for a reaction. Ruth had put a scruffy wig of varying colours on. They giggled like schoolgirls, pulling it all off as the waiter brought the bill then ran up the carpeted steps and onto the Royal Mile.

"Let's take a taxi, Ruth."

"But the place we want doesn't seem to have a name; we can't say – the narrow alley way please."

"No, but we can say the dock area, look, there's a taxi over there."

In the taxi, they had a look at the map; it showed a monument, so that's where they alighted. It didn't take long to discover the old alley way; both standing looking at it, neither liked the idea of venturing along the cobbles. Putting on their disguises, they made their way gingerly along the broken pathway. Helen pulled a hanky from her pocket and covered her mouth and nose. Looking at the crumbling wall surface and puddly ground with the smell of sewerage and fried food as they worked their way along was unpleasant.

Ruth was now linking her arm through Helen's and suddenly stopped. There were messages scratched on parts of walls and now and again what looked like the name of a building. Ruth was staring. Took at this and trying to read the words on an old decaying piece of wood, "Do you know where this is?" Helen shook her head. "This is the old quarter where the asylums were in the olden days; we are in the real old backstreets." The smell was getting worse and the trickle running along the cracks under their feet looked very suspicious.

"How do you know we are in the old asylum part, Ruth?"

Ruth pointed to a name. "That."

Helen went closer and tried to read the lettering. "Bedlam…bedlam."

"Yes, that's what they were called in the olden days; we learnt about it in college; do you know it's a later variation of Bethlehem? They were the first to start off places like this."

Not ever having been to college, Helen was a little surprised and not at all sure it was correct. A door suddenly opened lighting up the pathway as Helen and Ruth shrank back into the shadows. The figure started to urinate up the wall laughing to himself. The door closed, and they were in darkness again. "Oh, no, isn't that one of the names we are looking for?" Helen pointed above her head. The crudely painted sign, The Black Moon. "Shall we chance the back door?" Helen half-hoped Ruth would say no, but opening the door, they walked in. It was full of sour smoke, a couple of spittoons were on the floor, and Helen felt herself retch. Lifting her head momentarily, she managed to get a good look around. There were no other women that she could see and the men smiled at them saying something that Helen didn't understand. Hoping that Ruth was right behind her, she walked straight out the other end.

"I'm glad to be out of there."

"I suppose it seems worse in the dark." Helen didn't think it could be much better in the daylight. Now they were in the dockland area; they soon found the Tickling Trout, the pub with a very bad reputation, and they were heading right for it.

After being ungraciously pushed about, they managed to buy a drink. Looking around, any one of the rough men could have been a rustler, but they would just keep their eyes and ears open. Having bought half a pint of beer, they attempted to drink it while reading a grubby notice. "This was where the body snatchers operated from and did their deals, it's where the future doctors trained and practised on bodies they acquired."

"Ruth, don't tell me anymore. I shall have nightmares as it is." Working their way to the door and glad to be out in the air, they pulled their scarf, glasses and wig off. Hurrying along the dark street, Helen saw her maroon car and waited as the Rover pulled into the curb. "Lewis." Helen was so surprised she could hardly speak. "Get in and let's get out of this place."

Helen slipped into the back seat but Ruth jumped into the front seat saying, "Lewis, you're a star; how did you know where to pick us up?" He looked around at Helen.

"Lewis, this is Ruth; she's helping me find some clues." Later when they were well on their way home, Lewis told Helen that he was so worried about the area he knew they had gone to, that he just kept circling about it. Helen took the photo out of her bag and gave it to Ruth. "Did you see anyone like that tonight?" Ruth shook her head. "I think he has a wig on anyway." She sighed. "We had better make plans for the three county show, be lots of prize cattle there, Helen, that might bring them out. One of these days, we will have them."

"Yes, one day."

"Where am I dropping you off, young lady?"

"The car park at the top of the Royal Mile, thanks." Helen laid herself along the back seat and was soon fast asleep. Lewis took a slow ride back to the castle.

As far as Angus was concerned, things seemed to be coming together. He had a phone call from a detective in charge of theft of livestock letting him know that the area in question was now under surveillance twenty-four hours a day, as of yesterday. Also, a trap had been planned. They wanted to rid the highlands of this scourge, but it had to be kept hush-hush. "I'm only telling you this as a long standing trusted friend, Angus."

Today was the start of the three counties Live Stock Show. Already being able to hear the men working outside the bullpens, the cattle had been shampooed Helen guessed and now hearing the hoses going to rinse them off. A lot of work to be put in yet, telling herself she must remember her camera. A lot of deliberate movement had been going on in the grounds around the bullpens.

Chauffeur Lewis was waiting to take Helen to meet Ruth and then on to the show. A different cattle truck was parked in the centre of the castle grounds deliberately, and the newly acquired (decoy bull) Charles Henry with a pedigree of champions, and looking magnificent, was walked around then loaded.

There was a scuffle on the hillside as the trap had worked, and three men were handcuffed and led away. Angus had a phone call informing him of the arrest thanks to his visit to them with information. It was the children that discovered the lookout, no wonder the gang always knew what was going on. Angus and Mary drove over to the castle. Angus walked up to Stuart and slapping him on the back. "You needn't bother taking this fella to the show, lad; the show's over for the rustlers." And he told him what the police had said. Helen's car pulled out of the castle drive. With all the activity, she didn't see Mary and Angus and was now on her way to the show.

Checking in her handbag to make sure she had her camera and pulling out the photo Toby, the barman from Fay Island, had sent her, she studied it closely. At the top of The Royal Mile in Edinburgh, they stopped to pick Ruth up. Both women studied the photo. "Put it away, Helen, we don't want to look at his face for too long." Helen slipped it back in her bag. Something was bothering her. Ruth had suggested they move away from the show cattle. "That loud individual began to get on my nerves." Shaking out her long red hair and slipping her bag over her shoulder, she said, "Let's have a look in some of the tents," still feeling uneasy and not knowing why Helen agreed. Inside the Shetland wool garments on display, they admired the handy work of the women, next was a larger tent with lots of photos of highland cattle, the span of horns across their head enormous, and the ginger brown shaggy coats reminded them of how harsh the winter could be.

"Look at this, Ruth, a bull nose ring, and it says its real gold; now I've seen everything."

"Yeah, I bet."

There were many bottles of all descriptions from shampoos to cure all ails. Clippers, hoof trimmers, horn saws, very strong chains and right on the edge of the tent on a hook hanging from the roof was a very big ring of leather; it was rolled into circles getting thinner and thinner. The handle was finely plated backwards and forwards. Helen looked at it for a long time. "They don't use things like this now, do they," Ruth commented. Helen turned to her slowly shaking her head.

"Not where I live." Ruth thought Helen had a strange look on her face.

"Are you all right, Helen?" But she didn't seem to hear her; she was fingering the plated handle and looking at the roll of leather getting thinner and thinner with every turn until it split into a thong at the end with thin hard edges. "What a spiteful treatment for any animal."

"Where to now?" Helen looked at her watch.

"What about the refreshment tent?" They were still at the entrance to the tent when they noticed the mouthy show off they had moved away from earlier was there again, talking loudly above everyone else to impress his friends. Ruth was outside the small marquee, and every now and then, he would look across at her and say something that would impress the colourful attractive Ruth. Coming close to Helen, Ruth asked, "Did you hear what he said?"

"Yes." Helen watched the charade, thoughtful. Having heard him boasting loudly about being a crack shot, could hit any target over any long distance any time and sniggering a private joke with his friends, "not always the one I meant...." a burst of laughter

Both women looked at each other, realisation in their eyes. Helen knew an uncontrollable anger rising inside of her, feeling certain this was the man that shot Cavalier, possibly aiming for her husband. Robbing her son of his father and his beloved horse.

Not knowing where it had come from, she heard her voice shout out in a controlled manner. "You killed my husband." Suddenly, the people around were talking in a hushed whisper. Even louder this time. "I'm Helen McKlinross and you killed my husband James McKlinross, the laird of Bun Water Meet Castle."

Helen was aware of Ruth saying, "You snivelling little rattlesnake." He was looking wildly about having the attention he had been seeking was now worried.

"She's mad, you're mad," he said and shook a fist at her, drawing an ooh from the onlookers. Helen felt quite calm as she lifted down the bullwhip, handing her bags to Ruth.

"No, Helen, no, don't, leave it to the police." Then seeing the look on her face, Ruth called out, "Mind out the way." Then ducking smartly out of the way herself as Helen, with all her might delivered the first lash hitting its mark across cheekbone and forearm. The next caught him around the neck and stayed there for a moment making him scream.

"You killed my husband and now you are going to pay." Another vicious swipe with a resounding crack, which filled Helen with satisfaction and another swipe of stinging leather, this time there were several flecks of blood running down his face and arm.

He was screaming to the crowd, "Somebody stop her!" Nobody moved. Ruth could see two uniformed men running towards them and called out to Helen.

"Enough Helen…" Another powerful blow hit its mark.

The man was crawling now and begging someone to help. The two uniformed men were walking towards Helen as Ruth took the whip, partly rolling it up and walking backwards into the tent. "I'll take this." The woman held out a large bag. Hastily paying, dropping it behind the desk. "I'll be back" The woman pushed one of her cards into her hand.

Helen stood erect, unafraid. "He killed my husband." The two uniformed men redirected themselves to the man now being helped up.

"Well, well, well, it's you again." They looked him up and down. "And what have you been doing to upset the ladies?"

"She's mad I tell yer, mad," he said looking nervously at the two men that had hold of him now. "I didn't kill er usband. I swear I didn't; it was the horse…" He realised he had said too much. "How was I to know they would both fall off the rotten mountain?"

Two more uniformed men arrived and waited. Helen walked slowly up to him, but Ruth took her arm. "My son cried for years. We lost a truly wonderful man. He was a hardworking, kind man and you, you are a murderer."

As they turned and started to walk away, he almost spat the words at Ruth, "Ain't chew got anythin to say as well?" Ruth stopped and looked at him, stepping closer and smiling sweetly, taking a deep breath.

"Yes, actually I have." Bringing a hefty slap across his face and as he put his hands up to his face, her knee went in with a vicious jab causing him to double up in agony, now bent over in great discomfort and kneeling on the ground. Helen was smiling at Ruth who was grinning and nodding. "Good day's work."

"Okay, missy, that's enough now," indicating to the other two men who walked off with the girls. Ruth squeezed Helen's arm.

"I hope they put us in the same cell."

Chapter 28

Helen's maroon car followed them dutifully. The police car pulled into the police station, and Helen and Ruth were accompanied in by two uniformed officers. Inside was peaceful with just a couple of people waiting about. To Helen's surprise, she was walked along a short corridor and put into a small cell. Ruth was at the counter being questioned.

An hour later, Angus and Mary arrived. The officer behind the desk was reading through Ruth's statement as Angus approached. "Where is Mrs Mcklinross, officer?" Ruth came over to him.

"They've locked her up, can you believe it?" Angus looked at her pale face, then at the officer.

"On what charge?" He looked up from the paper.

"Oh, hello, Angus, haven't seen you in these parts for a while, erm…It's GBH."

"Is it possible to see her?" The officer came from behind the desk sorting some keys.

"I'll see what I can do" – with a quick wink – "follow me." Turning to Mary, he said, "Sorry, only one." They disappeared through the door. Mary went back to the counter where a younger officer was now reading through Ruth's statement.

"I don't suppose the poor lass has had a cup of tea." There was no response. "I tell ye, young man, if I had been there, I would have helped her to do this G B or whatever it is…" Without looking up, he said, "In that case, madam, you would be sharing her cell." He starts writing. "Go and sit down, there's a good girl."

The young man sitting quietly in the comer smiled to himself. Getting his notebook and pen out, he went and sat next to Mary and Ruth. Mary began talking to him straight away. After a while, getting her small photo book out, she proudly showed it to him. There were wedding, dance, castle, horses, lodge and prize bulls. "A reporter, you say, well, I think you should report this to whoever is in charge...higher up, mind you," she said not really grasping that he was a newspaper reporter from the Daily Scotsman.

"By the way, what is this G B... thing, do you have any idea?"

"It's GBH, means Grievous Body Harm, don't worry about it; she didn't look a dangerous lady to me." Ruth forgot herself for the moment.

"Huh, you didn't see her with the bull whip..." Raising his eyebrows, he opened his notepad again.

Angus joined them, and the young man asked him a few questions, but Angus was just a little more cautious with him. Ruth was free to go although she had been seen slapping the man's face, more discreet was the sharp kneeing causing him to double up. No way was she leaving without Helen.

The castle kitchen was warm and comforting. Katriana, Bryony, Molly and Ginty were sitting around the table sipping hot drinks worrying as to what was happening. Andrew and Stuart came in and Stuart started pouring drinks. "Come on, ladies, we need a pick me up after this shock." But he was laughing. "What about that then...that's my girl." He raised his arm above his head impersonating a whip cracking. The women looked at him not understanding his happy mood. Looking heavenwards, he paused from pouring and with gusto. "Can you hear me, James, are you not proud of her, my brother? It's okay; we've got it all in hand." He carried on pouring, with a knowing look at Andrew. "Drink up." The women looked from one to the other, completely baffled.

Molly fumbled in her pocket for her hanky. "But you don't seem to realise, our Helen is in prison...dear lord." She crossed herself and started to weep softly. Andrew went and stood behind her.

"It's all right, Molly; she's only in a police cell, drink up." Although he couldn't be a hundred per cent sure, but the two of them had contacted as many farmers and cattle breeders as they could, most had been victims of theft and were only too willing to join them. An hour later, they were on their way to the police station, six of them in the Land Rover.

Hoof beats announced the cattlemen arriving from checking the cattle and were also soon put in the picture, surprised at the actions of this gentle mild-natured woman's strength. They were all behind her. Telling the women to put the dinner back in the oven, they took off in the farm Land Rover.

When they reached the village, it wasn't possible to get close to the police station for the throngs of people reminding them of an old-fashioned film, with a posse, the cattle men were joking. A loud buzz of chatter filled the air, and there was a young man taking photos.

He was also chatting to people in the crowd and writing in his notebook. The men parked the Land Rover and walked to the police station acknowledging people they knew on their way. Stuart managed to talk his way into the police cell giving Helen a much needed hug. He was relieved to see she was fine and not ruffled in any way. In his usual joking way he said, "So they're not going to hang you this time…" Helen's expression darkened, and she looked down. Stuart took her hands and smiled at her shaking his head slowly. Looking directly at her, he saw just one small quiver of her lip. Her expression had changed, and for a moment, he was worried.

"Stuart, I know it was him. I wanted to kill him. I would have done if…" He pulled her into his arms.

"I hope you've got this out of your system now, my love." He felt her breathing shudder and loosened his hold. "Do you remember what we promised each other?" She looked up at him. "Well, I'm helping you now; we will get through it." He took a deep breath. "Have you any idea where they are keeping this person?" A broad grin spread across her tired face.

"He's in hospital."

Outside the police station, Andrew was surprising himself, hushing the crowd and telling them what he knew so far. "Mrs Helen Mcklinross says she is a hundred percent sure this is the man that shot Cavalier causing him to fall off the precipice killing both him and James." People in the crowd were calling out,

"She didn't kill anybody; why have they got her locked up – and where is this person now anyway?" A policeman came out of the door and tried to usher Andrew away, but instead, Andrew went into the police station. The crowd was growing bigger, and the police were telling them to go home; there was nothing to see, but nobody moved.

David Balantine and his stockman and the castle stockman were now standing close together. "Right, lads, a good old dose of Scottish persuasion, loud as ye can. We want Helen McKlinross; we want Helen McKlinross." The chant grew louder. Men that had worked alongside James and had great respect for him, Stuart acknowledged nodding to many. The light was fading, and it was beginning to get late, but still, the chanting went on. Suddenly, the large black door opened slowly; the crowd went quiet as Andrew, Helen, Stuart and Ruth came out into what daylight was left.

The crowd started cheering and calling out, "Well done – we are proud of you." It echoed in the valley and rebounded off the hills.

As they walked through the crowds to the Land Rover, they were shouting their thanks to the many people who had come along to support them. At the top of the hill, Helen could see her maroon car with Lewis and the boys everyone had been in on this. Helen felt so proud. Her and Ruth rode in the front to the tooting of horns until they were well out of the village.

James Junior lent into the front and hugged his mother and kissed her many times, along with the dog. Helen closed her eyes and revelled in the love. "Promise me you won't do anything like this again, Mum. Mary and Angus are at the castle now. Mary and Molly haven't stopped crying." The boys laughed.

"Yeah, they think you're locked up in prison." They sat back laughing again. Ruth turned to Helen.

"Oh dear, what are we going to do about your police record," she said trying not to laugh as she saw the boys' expression change, then winked at them. Helen turned to Ruth and was thoughtful for the moment.

They all waited, then, "You weren't exactly blameless. I know you gave him a slapping, but I saw that swift knee into his…" Lewis gave a discreet cough.

Leaning back, she knew she could relax. "Ruth, just think, we won't have to do this again." She had become used to the 'outings' with Ruth; she would miss her company.

"I dare say we will meet for coffee now and again. I would like that."

"Of course, you've got a court case to get through yet."

Putting her hand to her mouth, she said, "I'd forgotten all about that."

Smiling as he was driving, Lewis felt very proud of the family. Today, he had called Mrs McKlinross, Helen, for the first time since he had worked for her.

Dropping Ruth home first, they were now on their way to the castle. It had been a long and eventful day but a rewarding one. Helen knew it was wrong to be pleased with herself for badly injuring another human being, but she didn't consider him human, knowing she could have gone on for a lot longer doing him as much damage as she could.

As the car pulled in, the castle door burst open and first out was Mary and Angus. The boys and Lynnette tumbled out of the back of the car laughing and Helen and Baffles climbed wearily out of the front, with Lewis putting his arm under hers, which she was grateful for. Duncan dangled a pair of false handcuffs in front of Mary. "Look, Mary, we managed to get Auntie Helen's handcuffs off."

Throwing her hands up, she said, "Oh, you clever boy," amidst a burst of laughter.

It was good to sit in a comfortable seat and sip a hot drink. They were all talking at once, but Helen sat in the middle of it all and enjoyed the atmosphere.

When things had quietened down, Mary reminded her, "Do ye remember that it is David and Lucinda's moving day tomorrow, lass; will ye be comin to the lodge to see them off, about 2. Be nice if everyone came, just to give a wave." Helen nodded.

Opening her eyes to a shaft of sunlight, Helen lay enjoying the comfort of being back to normality. Calling out 'come in' to a knock on her bedroom door, it was Stuart's welcoming face. "This is a good start to the day, my handsome brother-in-law." Leaning over, she said, "Stuart, it's not even 6.30."

"I know but the fish man gave me a newspaper with the delivery. Helen, you've got to see this." Helen sat up as Stuart held up the front page for her to see. There was a full size photo of her and James and a large caption 'The Power of Love'.

A smaller picture was underneath of the crowds outside the police station. Helen gasped as she recognised many of the faces. Turning the page, there was a really good one of the castle. Under that was an impressive photo of three of the bulls and a star alongside one which said 'Still Missing'.

Covering her face with her hands, she stifled a sob. Stuart lowered himself to sit on the bed, gently taking her hands away. "It's a wonderful photo, Helen, look at it." They both sat looking at a large picture of James on Cavalier. She was not able to stop the tears that were now trickling down her cheeks.

"I loved him so much." Stuart put his arm around her shoulder.

"I know you did, my love." He took a deep breath. "I did too."

"Listen, I'm going to get some more papers. I'll be a little while; you get yourself ready and don't show this to anyone. When we are all in the kitchen, we will share this together. There's a big write up for you to read. I hope they've got all their facts right." He got up and kissed her head. "Now, please wait for me to get back. I'll be as quick as I can." He wiped her tears. "Scotland the Brave, see you downstairs later." At the bedroom door, he turned and looked at his brother's wife; she looked so sad now he wanted to hold her and kiss away her sadness. He closed the door quietly.

He stood for a moment thinking about his brother. "Well, James, as they say The Power of Love. You must be proud of her; it's been an uphill journey." Lately, he found himself often talking to his brother. It was a good feeling.

Stuart was sitting in the Land Rover reading a newspaper; there was a smile on his face. He had excitedly been to collect the papers early for everyone he could think of and was now on his way to deliver them. At Mount Eagle Place, dancing about on the step, Lucinda's maid answered the door looking adorable in her pink and white. "Give me a kiss then take this, tell them to read it straight away." The young woman took the newspaper then slowly lent towards him and planted a kiss full on his lips. Smiling sweetly, she closed the door, leaving a surprised Stuart looking bemused.

Pulling in at the lodge, he let himself into the kitchen to the homely aroma of coffee and fried bacon. Taking the tea towel from Mary and guiding her to a chair, he said, "Now, sit here and read this."

"Morning, Stuart, you're about early." Then she turned her attention to the paper. Stuart waited long enough to see her face change.

"I've got to go. I'm paperboy at the moment." And he went out into the garden with Mary close behind.

Smiling to himself, as he heard Mary's voice, "Angus McGregor, come in this minute."

He drove to the castle surveying the lush fields and being thankful for the privileged place he lived. Opening the windows, he breathed deeply, seeing the morning sun playing on the lake like a sunbeam that he felt he could almost slide down into the water. Pulling up outside the outer pens, he jumped out and handed the stockman two papers. "Break time…this has made my day." At the castle door, he looked around and waved as he heard a shout go up.

Entering the kitchen, he hung his head looking forlorn. Molly looked at him and immediately searched for her hankie. Crossing herself, she said, "Oh, dear lord, has our Helen got herself a criminal record." They all paused with cups in the air as if frozen in time. Hurriedly putting the mood right and dropping the stack of newspapers onto the table, Stuart gave over to Andrew who read steadily and the listeners relaxed.

"Scotland the Brave. How good to know the Scottish people still hold fast to the bravery bestowed on them by their forefathers and stand together. This is the story of Mrs Helen McKlinross of Watersmeet Castle, who lost her husband in a tragic way while hunting the rustlers with other cattle owners.

"Mrs McKlinross has never given up looking for James McKlinross's killer and told the police many times she would be able to recognise one of the men who stole his champion bull 'Out Of The Blue'. The man or men that knocked her out causing her to have many bruises and stitches to her head." Andrew looked about him at the attentive faces. Molly sniffed and put her hankie away. Stuart had arranged a tray of glasses and a bottle of whisky on a tray, with a frown from Katriana.

"Now come on, Mother, we are going to do this properly, right, carry on, Andrew." Bryony suddenly jumped off her chair.

"Wait a minute, I don't want to miss a word." And she disappeared, appearing a few minutes later with cake, selection of biscuits and sweets. As Stuart poured, Bryony handed plates around and cut cake. Stuart smiled and winked at her 'that's my girl' as Andrew resumed the story. Ginty passed the plates along, looking spellbound.

A few minutes later, the phone rang and Duncan went to answer it. "It's for you, Auntie Helen."

"We will wait for Helen, drink up." But after ten minutes, Katriana went to see what the holdup was. Coming back into the kitchen, she shrugged her shoulder.

"Helen says to carry on."

"Do you think she might be some time, Mother?" Katriana smiled at her son.

"Yes, it's the press."

Stuart kept eye on the time. "Mother, better remind Helen we are supposed to be waving the Balentines off at two o'clock; the press will keep her talking all day."

At two o'clock on the dot, the two removal lorries moved off with David and Lucinda following behind in their huge white Mustang American car. They had been very good and generous neighbours to Angus and Mary, and Helen knew she would miss them greatly. David's wine had been drunk and now Lucinda was waving a lace hankie with a royal nod now and then, which brought a cheer. Helen had let them take quite a lot of antiques as she knew she would be needing the room, including the suite of armour that Lucinder was passionate about, knowing there were two in the castle.

The following morning, Stuart was at the newsagent's first thing. Chatting to the same man he saw at the police station. The editor was very keen to do a follow up story as they had lots of interest now in what was going on in the castle.

The news man told him, who turned out to be 'Nigel with the News' that they would like to run a weekly story covering Helen's life story, with a peep into castle life and those involved in it.

For once, Helen didn't consult any one for advice, as she knew that she wanted to tell her story, their undying love story. Helen wanted the world to know about the man she loved and lost and set about putting it on to paper. This turned out to be the start of something big. Turning to her photos, she started her story with their meeting by the burn all those years ago and each week touched on highlights of their life, how he constantly rode the boundaries as the rustling became worse and how he helped the outlying farmsteads.

There was so much to tell, and running the dance school in between was difficult. Both James Junior and Lynnette were pupils; their ballet surprised everyone. At first, Duncan and Robert thought it a great laugh but after seeing a performance had nothing but admiration. Neither of them wanted to join the classes.

After a few months, they noticed cars coming to the castle gates, taking photos and driving away. 'Nigel with the News' told Helen there was a holiday tour company wanting to see her about setting up conducted tours to the many places of interest that had appeared in Helen's weekly stories, like the bullpen of the now famous 'Out of the Blue'. They wanted to see the magnificent Cavalier's resting place with his statue. Great interest was now shown in the area where the stone mounds were and the cleit where James was buried. Helen began to feel perhaps she had aroused too much interest in more personal places and cleverly steered the interest towards Fay Island with its wonderful observatory and her stories of the Sentinel. Helen wrote to Toby the bartender who had been a great help in her recognising James's killer, not knowing whether they minded her mentioning the story of McTavish and Lilly, telling her to go ahead.

It was like opening the floodgates, things were happening so fast. There were fifty different postcards, one even of the four children now called the 'Castle Cavaliers'. It had turned into a real business venture and the revenue was very rewarding.

Stuart and Andrew had started selling the livestock and just kept a few top animals from the prize stock. Life was much easier for them now. No need to ride the boundaries as both being semi-retired gave a lot of their time entertaining tourists creating many laughs.

The dance school was now flourishing and boasted six tutors covering all kinds of dance, even ballroom, aptly taught in part of the ballroom. Helen still wrote her weekly story interest enjoying the mail she received. Not everyone was happy with the tourists as some of the letters showed. Everyone enjoyed more relaxation time and were always going here and there driven by Helen's chauffeur, the attractive Lewis.

Not feeling quite herself this morning again, she stood looking at her sketch from yesterday on her upright easel but wasn't tempted to carry on with it. It was from memory of a handsome ginger beige long-coated highland cow just going over the ridge of a hill with the setting sun turning half of her orange gold. Looking around the clustered walls, her many photos over the years enlarged and framed, her eyes picked out the photo on Fay Island. Smiling to herself, yes, she remembered getting lost on the hills when photographing. Thinking often over the years she would have liked to go back there, possibly have another ride in Blondie, wondering if the little open-air jeep was still about. It was a nice thought.

Looking at her high-arched door, which, over the years, she had used to create some stunning life-sized paintings was the wonderful Cavalier, James's horse. Yes, this was her masterpiece. The large intelligent eyes seemed to follow her around the room, lifting her head to look up into them. Her fingers traced along the back of the white dog she had painted, coming back from Fay Island. Lilly was sitting on a grass-covered boulder just as she remembered her; she was very real, wondering where the clay pipe was now as she had left it on the bar shelf along with the dressing gown. It seemed a long time ago. Remembering the happiness and love.

Turning back to the oblong turret window and immediately losing herself in the hypnotic vista, she slowly rubbed her arms. The ache seemed to be there almost all the time now, but the view from this height she was never tired of. Looking now through the telescope would make her feel better.

In the castle kitchen, dinner was being prepared for the evening, and Molly was organising morning coffee tea and cake. The cattlemen and gardeners would be in soon, and they looked forward to this. All the family were home as it was the weekend so there was a lot of chatter and laughing. Bryony was cutting generous portions of cake and Ginty was pouring the drinks as the men came in to the kitchen with gusto. Andrew went and sat by his wife drying his hands and

Stuart had to retrieve the towel from him, snatching it good naturedly and flicking him with it.

"Why do we only have one towel in this kitchen," he grinned knowing he was winding Molly up.

"You little heathen, you know you wash yaysel in the basin in there," she said pointing to the special washroom that the others were dutifully using. "You behave yasel, Stuart McKlinross, or you will go to your room…" This brought a burst of laughter.

Helen leaned into the telescope. Like glass, the water below shone, gentle movement making white edged lines appear and disappear. Tiredness enveloped her as it had been doing often these last few weeks, and she fought the urge to lay on her inviting bed sofa. Looking at her watch, it was time to meet up in the kitchen, but the crystal clear view of the distant mountains and the sight of a seal surfacing and pulling itself onto the stony shore…The sky directly above was blue but powdery. Some white clouds further away resting on mountaintops made the mountains shadowy. Some geese from the lake flew up passing the turret window quite close, their outline dark with the sun behind them. Helen mused how nice it would to be able to fly, as she lowered herself onto the large soft cushions, drifting off into a light sleep. If only the ache in her arms would go, she would be very comfortable.

Molly, looking at Stuart and Andrew, said, "Will you no go and fetch the turret girls and tell them it's on the table." She referred to Helen and Katriana ever since they liked spending time in their respective turrets. "They've always got their head in the clouds these days tch…" Just at that moment, Katriana came in, smiling.

"Good timing, Mother, you're looking pleased with yourself," Stuart said pulling a chair out for her.

Picking a serviette up and placing it across her lap daintily, she replied, "I am pleased with myself. I've just finished putting together another photo album."

"Oh, no, you've not put the one of me on the sheepskin rug with no clothes on, have you, Mother?" Kissing Bryony lightly on the cheek and smiling, he added, "I was only a few weeks old."

Katriana, helping herself to a portion of butter and a scone smiled to herself correcting him, "Ten months old."

Seeing Molly's finger wagging at him. "Okay, I'm going."

"And don't hurry her, Stuart; she's looked a might fragile lately. I've got her favourite butter shortbread."

Helen's eyes opened slowly, still feeling very sleepy. Thinking she hears a dog bark, she smiles. "Is that you, Lilly?" Finding it difficult to raise herself up on her arms, she half closes her eyes seeing Cavalier move and look as if he's walking towards her as Stuart quietly and slowly opens the door. Feeling radiant, she whispers, "Is that you, Cavalier, have you brought James to me?" Stuart comes alongside her.

"Helen…" She smiles raising her arms slightly, her voice a whisper.

"Oh, James, I knew you would come back for me one day, my darling James." Stuart slides his arms around her. "James, I love you so much. I'm glad you're here." Helen feels herself being lifted up and thinks it is into James's arms to ride with him like they used to. "I feel like I am floating." Stuart feels her suddenly stiffen, as her head rolls into his shoulder. Stuart holds her close and kisses her hair.

"Helen, Helen," he says feeling a wave of panic. "No, Helen, don't leave us." He looks at the face of the woman he has a great affinity for and knows she has gone.

Laying her back down, he kneels by the silent figure and sobs. "James, she thought I was you. I'm sure she's with you now," he says wiping his eyes. "I did my best after you were gone…you…and Dad. I didn't think I could go on," he said stroking the soft hair. "But she helped me…" he continued laying his head on the bed next to her now letting himself cry unashamed.

In the kitchen, he stood at the door. "Mother…could you…" His face slowly crumpled. "Helen is dead." He sat down at the table lowering his head and sobbed. Katriana and Molly, horror struck, went quietly out of the door. Bryony slowly shook her head in disbelief.

"No, no she can't." She put her arm around Stuart. Ginty went into Andrew's arms. They were all in shock; it was so unexpected. The workmen filed out respectfully, saying if there was anything they could do to help, just say. Andrew looked at his cousin; they had all loved Helen; she had been a bright light in their lives.

Andrew, his hand on Stuart's shoulder said, "It's all right. I'll go to the studio and tell James Junior. I don't think I'll phone." Taking Ginty's hand, he said, "Come with me." Andrew looked at Lewis's pale face. "Give me ten minutes then bring the car around." Lewis nodded and went out. He sat in the car, heartbroken. Pulling the cap down his face, he cried into the soft lining, feeling a cold nose pushed into his face as Baffles climbed onto his lap and licked his tears.

They drove in silence to Eagle Mount Place, except for Ginty's stiffled sobs. Wiping her eyes, she said, "They will be in the middle of a performance; it's their last night." Pulling in, they sat for a while and collected themselves.

Lynnette saw Andrew and Ginty come through the door to the backstage; she smiled delightedly and went forward to let them know James was just about to go on stage for his solo dance and to usher them into the wings to watch. "James will surprise you, he is so good." Her face held such pride and excitement. "Watch for his opening leap and the height he reaches; he's incredible." Andrew and Ginty looked at each other and Ginty slipped her arm around Lynnette's shoulder.

The music rose to a crescendo as the brilliant spotlight lit the leaping figure that seemed to hover in space for a few seconds. The audience gasped in appreciation as spinning and leaping, strong but graceful, James worked in a circle around the stage with breath-taking moves, the split leaps and stag jumps so perfectly performed, coming to an end with a knee spin, his arms outstretched, exactly on the note. His handsome face shining with happiness the image of his father as he lifted it to the clapping audience.

James went straight to Lynnette, his voice an excited whisper. "Lynnette, something really strange happened on my entrance, that's the highest I've ever reached in a jump, but the spotlight…" He paused, as she smiled and took his hand. "For a split second, I thought I saw my mother and father, and they were smiling." Keeping hold of his hand, she turned him towards Andrew and Ginty.

Stroking the back of his hand, she said, "They've something to tell you."